APPARITIONS

APPARITIONS

A Historical Novel

BY

Begoña Echeverria

This book was published with generous financial support from the Basque Government.

Center for Basque Studies
University of Nevada, Reno
1664 North Virginia St,
Reno, Nevada 89557 usa
http://basque.unr.edu

ISBN-13 9781949805895 (paperback) | ISBN-13 9781949805901 (epub)

Series: Basque Originals Series #31

Cover image credit: Obreras del hogar: acudid todas a la conferencia que se celebrará el día 3 en el salón teatro de la Casa del Pueblo" by Cantos, ca. 1937. Used with permission by Fundación Pablo Iglesias.

Printed in the United States of America

Library of Congress Cataloging-in-Publication Data

Names: Echeverria, Begoña, author.

Title: Apparitions : a historical novel / by Begoña Echeverria.

Description: Reno : Center for Basque Studies, University of Nevada, 2024. | Series: Basque original series ; 31 | Summary: "In the mystical backdrop of the Pyrenees, young Blanca's life takes a dramatic turn when she experiences a divine apparition of the Virgin Mary. Set in the turbulent 1930s Basque Country, Apparitions intertwines historical events with spiritual mysticism, as Blanca is chosen to deliver a message of hope amidst impending doom. As political tensions rise and the threat of war looms, Blanca must navigate her newfound role while grappling with the weight of her visions. Her journey is one of faith, family, and the struggle to do what is right in a world where the lines between reality and the supernatural blur. Echeverria crafts a poignant narrative that delves deep into the intersection of religion, tradition, and the personal challenges of a young girl thrust into extraordinary circumstances. Will Blanca be able to heed the Blessed Mother's call and protect her loved ones, or will the darkness of war consume them all? Apparitions is a compelling tale of courage, political awakening, and the enduring power of belief"— Provided by publisher.

Identifiers: LCCN 2024038068 (print) | LCCN 2024038069 (ebook) | ISBN 9781949805895 (paperback) | ISBN 9781949805901 (epub)

Subjects: LCSH: Basques—Fiction. | Mary, Blessed Virgin, Saint—Apparitions and miracles—Fiction. | Mysticism—Fiction. | País Vasco (Spain)—History—20th century—Fiction. | LCGFT: Historical fiction. | Novels.

Classification: LCC PS3605.C34 A88 2024 (print) | LCC PS3605.C34 (ebook) | DDC 813/.6—dc23/eng/20240909

LC record available at https://lccn.loc.gov/2024038068

LC ebook record available at https://lccn.loc.gov/2024038069

Aranzibia Hill, Indartze, the Pyrenees

27 iúil, 1931

July 27, 1931

I reach the summit of the apparition site, Aranzibia Hill, and cannot believe the transformation since I came here last, some forty days ago. Though the encircling mountains burst with foliage, the four slender oaks have been stripped of their leaves and their bark chiseled off. The naked trees look like waifs or strays that barely survived the Great War. The grass and sunflowers have been stamped out. Where a simple cross and rudimentary altar once stood now stretches up a sturdy roof, from which sways a garland of roses shaped into the letter *M*. Adorning the altar are rose petals, thistles like those fastened on front doors to ward off witches, and funeral cards, photographs, and small pieces of paper with petitions on them. Canes and shepherds' crooks peek out from under the vesperal cloth. All the visitors up here seem to be wearing a religious medallion around their necks and holding a Bible in their hands, even small children and adults I know cannot read. I wonder if my long-lost love is here, and what I would say—should say—if I see her, after everything that's happened.

Flashbulbs pop, aggravating my migraine.

The dusk punctuated by little lights burning like fairy lamps in the woods, I can see tens of thousands of people have gathered. They come from all walks of life: men in three-piece suits and fedoras; women in tailored dresses and knitted caps covering their fashionably short brown hair; peasant men in navy blue cotton pants and linen shirts, their sleeves rolled up to the elbows; farm women clothed in simple dresses in muted colors. Of course, members of the clergy abound. A gaunt monk dressed in a black soutane leads them; his is the cavernous face of an Inquisitor. Even the young children await the spectacle. A photographer has set up a stand, and a brunette, whose hair had been Marcel-waved to perfection, wears a fox stole draped over her black dress. She poses near the "vision grove."

Down below, a parade of coaches, automobiles, pony traps, private motors, mule-driven carts, motorcyles, and buses wend their way up the dirt path to the base of the mountain. On my ascent, I noticed a 1930 Madame X Sedan Cabriolet with diplomatic plates. A dozen passengers spill out of a white bus, their luggage piled on the roof. Some immediately follow their priest to join the people ascending to the hilltop; others mill about the stalls seeking mementos. The noxious vapor of skunks and incense returns my attention to those near me at the peak, where a gray-haired man in a beret does brisk business selling chestnuts, his customers chatting amiably as they await their treat. Here and there, I see middle-aged women selling caramels, biscuits, postcards, rosaries or plastic bottles shaped in the image of the Virgin Mary. My musician's ear detects among the crowd snatches of intense whispers in Basque, Castilian, and French. The collective excitement is profound, yet my heart goes out to all these people and the disappointment they will certainly feel when this is all over.

Many climb over the wire rails surrounding the stark trees. One woman, kissing the oaks, says they are a sign from God symbolizing the four provinces of the Basque Country: Navarra, Gipuzkoa, Bizkaia, and Araba (I know from living in Bayonne that Basques there would take offense at the exclusion of their home province). Men take off their caps as they reach the summit. I feel their remonstrance at my broad straw hat. I keep it on lest people recognize me, for I fear I could not endure a repeat of their violence. Though my scraggly beard may not sufficiently obscure the knife wound on my cheek, I hope it will not attract attention in this new world of "stigmata" suffered by the seers.

Young girls hum as they sprinkle onto the path rose petals from small baskets they carry. Some stoop to gather strawberries, which they slip into their mouths. As one reaches for mushrooms that have sprouted after the recent rains, a woman slaps the child's hand away. "Those are the bad ones!" she says in Castilian. Her black hair and dark eyes contrast sharply with her pale skin. She is dressed in a smart, dark blue costume, her hands encased in gray kid gloves. "They'll make you see things." She takes a plastic bottle from her coat pocket and pours water over the girl's hands. "This will protect you. It's from the spring."

As if on cue, the roar of the spring rushes through my ears, momentarily drowning out the cacophony from the crowd.

A great many infirm have made the climb, desperately seeking the spring's magic: Three young men and a stocky woman carry a paralytic on a stretcher; lame men and children hobble alongside them. Blind men holding long sticks trudge up the hill, some with little boys to guide them, one led by a dog on a leash. They lumber along, groaning as they make their slow climb. A man wearing a bronze medal from Spain's Morocco campaign is missing both legs. Sweating profusely, he uses his powerful arms to push himself along on a board affixed with wheels.

A dozen young men dressed entirely in black and wearing the telltale red beret with the yellow tassels of the Acción Católica charge up the hill like soldiers determined to defend their territory. Yet, young boys tumble over one another, laughing. A woman in a widow's black dress and mantilla mutters under her breath, "*Jesús mío!* For them it's a big party!"

The widow falls to her knees as the sun sinks into the horizon. The chattering dies down and everyone kneels. I join them, though not a believer. I wince as I land in a rut. My knees throb in pain; the arduous climb has inflamed the injuries I sustained from the attack earlier. One of the widows begins to pray the Rosary in Basque.

Agur Maria graziaz betea	Hail Mary, full of grace
Jauna da zurekin	The Lord is with you
Bedeinkatua zare	Blessed are you
Emazte guzien artean	Among women
Eta benedikatua da	And blessed is the fruit
Zure sabeleko fruitua Jesus	Of your womb, Jesus

The people answer back, even the rowdy boys, just as the chorus answers me when I play the Caoineadh lament on my fiddle. I close my eyes and sway to the rhythm, hoping for a distraction from the pain shooting up my spine.

Maria saindua Jainkoaren Ama	Holy Mary, Mother of God
Egizu otoiz gu bekatorarentzat	Pray for us sinners
Orai eta gure heriotzeko orenean	Now and at the hour of death
Halabiz	Amen

They sing the verses over and over. The monotony hypnotizes me into drowsiness despite my intensely uncomfortable position. I long to stand but dare not in the face of so many women and elderly praying as still as statues on the uneven hilltop. The pilgrims keep track of the decades on their rosary beads in one hand, striking their chests with the other. Every now and again they look to the sky anxiously. The air becomes humid. High above the trees in front of me, I see a thin white line snake across the sky. I look around and wonder if anyone else has noticed it. The crowd begins the Litany in Latin: *"Rosa mys-tica, Turris Davidica, Turris eburnea, Domus aurea."* The words resound in the darkening sky studded with stars. I feel the devotional excitement of these thousands and thousands of people envelop me and lift up my spirit.

"Le veo! I see her!" A cry pierces through the buzzing rhythm of the Litany.

It is Blanca, the ten-year-old girl everyone has waited for. She has edged her way through the crowd without my noticing and stands near me. She wears a white muslin dress with a light cape over it, the white ribbon on her short black hair illuminated by the tall candles beside the altar and those held by the pilgrims. Her face is so transformed it becomes exquisite. Bartolomé Esteban Murillo would have found in her the model for the faces of the angels in his inspired canvases.

A blizzard of languages floods in from the crowd:

"Does the Blessed Mother have a message?"

"I don't see anything."

"You have to believe to see her!"

Blanca falls to her knees in the dirt, disregarding the folded *Le Matin* and *Gure Txoko* newspapers the devout have placed there to keep her skirt clean.

"The vision!" a man with a thick Catalan accent shouts. "It's coming!"

Blanca stretches out her arms as if she's hanging on a cross and tilts her head, eyes fluttering.

"The Virgin Mary sits on a throne, holding the baby Jesus on her lap," she says in a thin, high-pitched voice.

By now Blanca knows the multitude hungers for details.

"Her crimson robe drapes over her flowing gown, embroidered with gold," she says. "A king with black hair kneels before her with his blond queen!"

This sounds like the painting of *The Virgin of the Catholic Monarchs* I've seen at the Prado Museum in Madrid; Isabel and Ferdinand are praying before the Virgin, receiving divine approval for their conquests abroad. There's no way Blanca would know this image on her own.

"The miracle will soon be upon us," Blanca says. "The Virgin will appear with three angels, a half-moon at her feet! An extraordinary radiance will light up the entire mountain! Some will see the Virgin, others only her shadow, still others nothing at all. The miracle will be seen on Aranzibia Hill but will be noted by the entire world. Afterward, the world will be at peace, the people content and blessed, because prayer will reign."

Blanca falls silent but moves her lips as she keeps focused on the four great oaks surrounding her. Only a woodpecker's strike against the tallest oak can be heard as the pilgrims hold their breath.

"She has told me the day the miracle will come," Blanca says. "On that day, the good will be welcomed into heaven, and I hope to be among them!"

More questions sprinkle in from believers:

"Please tell us the day!"

"What must I do to join you in heaven?"

"Blessed are you, Blanca!"

A gust of wind kicks up, and with it come comments from the skeptics:

"That's the witches' wind from the north!"

"She's making this up to get attention!"

"Isn't she the girl who hurt her head?"

"She's gone mad!"

"I will not tolerate such blasphemy against this girl!" The monk has made his way to Blanca's side. "She has been chosen as a divine messenger."

Blanca stays focused on the vision, and her face transforms once again. Fear burns in her eyes as she struggles to speak. "Twenty-five angels surround the Virgin Mary, their swords drawn," she says. "Saint Michael holds the biggest sword of all. It drips with blood! She wipes the blood with a white cloth."

I tremble at this image, so different from the loving Blessed Mother in Blanca's early visions.

Without warning, Blanca falls against me and her body quivers as if a great shock goes through her. I hold her, my hands large against her frail back. She tosses her arms about and tries to jump to her feet. She keeps slipping back to the ground as though an unseen power pushes her down. The crowd calls out. Blanca's body tenses as she listens and speaks to her vision. Her cheeks and forehead redden; her skin feels warmer to the touch, as if a fever were coming upon her. Her Virgin Mary reliquary pendant burns her neck, but she doesn't react.

The rowdy boys start crying, calling out to their own mothers.

Then Blanca stands up and points to a spot above the four towering trees. The woodpecker flies away. Blanca clenches her hands and speaks in a low and gravelly voice: "There will be civil war in the Basque Country between Catholics and unbelievers. We will suffer severely and lose many men at first. In the end, the righteous will triumph with the help of the Blessed Mother's twenty-five angels."

Strong emotions erupt from the crowd—whether out of fear or rhapsody, I cannot tell. The lame and crippled weep openly. Some children join in the crying, others break into song. The widows fall back onto their knees and pray with the rosaries clutched in their hands. The great concourse of people murmurs excitedly: the young and old; the fair and ugly; the ill and the well; aristocrat and peasant; priest and parishioner; zealots like my long-lost love and skeptics like me.

Sheer terror immobilizes me. The energy emanating from Blanca reaches me, and I feel my pain dissipate. I am too afraid to look at the sky where she has pointed lest I too see the vision and hear the message. Forcing myself to look up—for a second—I see the sky slowly open up, pierced by a strange light. Blanca falls back, her eyes staring, her mouth open. I touch her wrist and feel a slight pulse. Blanca's face is the color of wax, yet her expression suggests she beholds something astonishing.

CHAPTER ONE

Aranzibia Hill, Indartze, the Pyrenees

1930eko azaroaren 8a
November 8, 1930

Blanca held a basket with one hand and her father's arm with the other as he leaned on his cane. She could go up Aranzibia Hill faster on her own, but she welcomed the slower pace and the chance to spend more time alone with Aita.

She enjoyed the quiet as well. Every now and again she heard a bird chirp or leaves rustling, but mostly she and Aita walked through silence. "The animals like to nap too," her father liked to say.

Blanca's father tapped his walking stick at the bend in the path where the dirt road turned up toward the hill. She helped him take a seat on a stump from a tree he had felled last year.

"Try the meadow by that oak grove." He pointed to the top of the hill. "I'd wager you'll find good mushrooms there."

Blanca clapped her hands, her basket swinging.

"Ready?" Aita asked, the familiar twinkle in his eye.

Blanca readied herself at the foot of the narrow path worn by their weekly ritual.

"*Bat, bi, hiru,*" her father called out. "One, two, three . . ."

"Go!" Blanca yelled the command with her father, charging up Aranzibia Hill, doing her best to keep the hem of her skirt from grazing the dirt, moist from yesterday's rain. Breathing hard from the effort, she heard Aita's encouragement grow fainter and fainter. The sweet smell of wild roses urged her forward.

"Keep going," he called out. "The king of the mushrooms awaits!"

A crow cawed. The trees grew taller and taller as she approached the grove. She stayed in their shade to avoid the snakes that might be sunning themselves.

She reached the four oak trees, leafy and tall, and signaled to her father by waving her basket. Wiping the sweat from her face with her apron, she saw clusters of mushrooms peeking through the lush grass.

"You're right again!" Blanca cried out, though her father likely couldn't hear her. "There's a bunch here!" *It's like magic,* she thought. *He always knows where the good ones are.*

He'd shown her how to tell the good and bad mushrooms apart last summer, when he could still make the climb. The good ones felt firm to the touch, their insides fine and smooth. The bad ones—destroying angels and death caps—had rotten stems and felt spongy and soft on the inside.

"You must not touch those," he'd said, his voice serious. "They can make you sick. They can make you see things and put us in great danger." He paused. "We're going to pick only the good ones. And then I'll fry them up for us with eggs and garlic."

Blanca's mouth watered at the thought. She turned her attention to the mushrooms underfoot. Crouching with her skirt tucked under her bottom, Blanca looked for the deep bronze color atop the *onddo beltza*—the "black mushrooms" with the fat white stems. Their dark outsides yielded to white, meaty insides that looked like silk when cooked. She picked one after another, filling her basket.

She heard the wind whisper through the trees and looked up to see a white dove soaring overhead.

Oh! I wonder if it's telling me to look up there!

The dove rested on a branch on the tallest oak tree. The sun shone through the white of its feathers as it flapped its wings.

Her eyes fixed on the dove, Blanca felt dizzy, as she had a few days ago when she fell down the stairs and hit her head.

The shape of the bird melted into the patchy clouds in the blue sky, forming what appeared to be a face. She squinted. Now she could see a woman's face, framed with long flaxen hair. The woman wore a flowing gown of cornflower blue. The baby she cradled reached for the white rose she held. The woman kissed the top of the baby's head, then smiled at Blanca.

Blanca fell to her knees, dropping her basket, and made the sign of the cross and whispered, "Ama Maite Maria."

She bowed, touching her forehead to the earth.

"Blanca," the Blessed Mother said. "My child, I have come to give you a message."

"Yes, Ama?" Blanca clasped her hands together, eager to absorb the Blessed Mother's words.

"Ignore the foolishness of this world and do what is right and true," she said. Do this, and in heaven you will be welcomed by a choir of angels."

"*Bai, Bai!*" Blanca said. "I will! I will!"

"Evildoers will soon engulf Spain." A cloud darkened the Blessed Mother's brow. "She will burn like the fires of hell. You must help my people: *Gaizkatu Herria.*"

"*Bai,* Ama Maite Maria," Blanca said, more quietly this time. "But how? What must I do?" She didn't know what *gaizkatu* meant yet didn't feel she could ask. Fear overwhelmed her at the thought of these evildoers. Who could they be? Would they really burn everything up? What could a young girl like her do to stop them?

Just as suddenly, the worry left her. The sun shone its rays behind the Blessed Mother's head so brightly Blanca had to close her eyes. Her whole being filled with peace. She wept with joy at being chosen for this mission. But she also felt anxious that she wouldn't do it right.

Tilting her head toward the vision, she prayed with all her heart: "Oh, Blessed Mother, give me the strength to do what's right and true."

"I shall come to you again, my child." The Blessed Mother looked upon her with such love that Blanca thought she'd burst with it. "You will find me when you need me."

A monk vulture shrieked overhead. It caught the white dove in its huge, black-tipped beak and disappeared with it behind the trees.

The Blessed Mother, too, had vanished from the sky. A stillness now enveloped Aranzibia Hill and the surrounding valley. Blanca stood, astonished at what she'd heard and seen.

"Blanca!" Aita's hoarse voice pierced the silence. "Come down! Your mother will be waiting!"

Blanca shook her head and rubbed her eyes. Had she been dreaming? There was not a thing in the clear blue sky, and the only sound she heard was her father's voice.

"*Heldu naiz,*" she called out. "I'm coming." She raced down the hill.

"Blanca!" Aita rose from the tree stump. "What took you so long?" He eyed her closely and asked more gently, "What happened to you up there? Your clothes are rumpled and you forgot the basket. Your face looks . . . different."

"Something did happen, Aita!" Blanca caught her breath. "A miracle: the Blessed Mother appeared to me!"

"What?" Aita sounded worried.

Blanca took her father by the arm, steadying him. "Our Blessed Mother, she came to give me a message. She said—"

"—*Ixo, neska!* Be quiet, girl!" He looked around, drew her tighter, and put a finger to his lips. "Your hands got dirty. Did you touch those bad mushrooms? The death caps?"

Blanca remembered the mushrooms she'd picked. Should she go find the basket to show him?

"She really came to me," Blanca said. "She told me—"

"—I said be quiet!" His voice rose in anger.

Blanca was used to this tone only from her mother.

"What you saw, think you saw, you cannot tell a soul. It could be dangerous to you, to us, if people found out."

What could be dangerous about the Blessed Mother and doing good against evil?

"Yes, Aita," she said. "I'll do as you say."

"Good." He squeezed her hands. "It wouldn't be the first time a young girl in our family suffered for having seen things, real or not. We can't let that happen to you."

"I will tell no one." Blanca bit her lip. *Who was this girl Aita was talking about?*

It had been a week since she had seen the Blessed Mother, and Blanca longed to tell someone. Aita had looked at her sternly and chatted more than usual when the family ate together, as though he didn't trust her to hold her tongue.

Blanca didn't understand what could be wrong with telling people about the Blessed Mother's visit. Ama led the family in the Rosary every night, and the priest often closed Mass by leading the congregation in a song to the Blessed Mother. They always asked her to "pray for us." Why would she not come in person to answer those prayers?

Every night, Blanca tried to do what the Blessed Mother had asked. Or the part she understood: to do what was right and true. She wrapped around her fingers the wooden rosary Aita had made and prayed for her family. She prayed Aita's pain would go away so that he could walk as easily as he used to. She prayed Ama would worry less about how to make ends meet. She prayed for her brother, Cruz, too. He seemed content enough, though she sensed a restlessness in him she prayed would go away. Sometimes Blanca would even pray for herself: That she would be worthy of the Blessed Mother's trust in her. And that she would figure out what *gaizkatu* meant so that she could carry out that part of the mission, even though it sounded scary.

The Blessed Mother came to Blanca in her dreams every night, so Blanca knew her vision on Aranzibia Hill was real. When Blanca got up and opened the shutters to let in the sunshine, with it came another vision. This time the apparition had dark brown hair and wore a dark blue gown. Little angels floated around her.

"Your mother is proud, my child," the Blessed Mother said. "But also hurt. Her life did not turn out as she had hoped."

The words hit Blanca like a blow to the chest. "Is she disappointed in me?"

The Blessed Mother took Blanca's hands in hers. "No, she wanted you very much. She prayed and prayed to me for you after having lost many babies."

Blanca had no idea. That would explain Ama's frequent dark moods. And why Cruz was so much older than she was.

"Then why is she so cold to me?" Blanca teared up

The Blessed Mother wiped Blanca's cheeks. "Sadness and loss have hidden her heart. You can help her find it again." The Blessed Mother's image began to fade. "Remind her of the carefree girl she used to be before she became a wife and mother. What used to bring light to her eyes."

"I've never seen her like that," Blanca said. "What should I do?"

But the Blessed Mother was gone. Blanca fell to her knees and prayed she would have the patience to wait for the answer.

A knock interrupted her prayers. She opened the door. At the threshold sat a package wrapped in burlap.

"Oh!" she thought aloud. "What can this be?"

She carefully picked up the object, brought it into her room, and gingerly untied the leather string. "Oh, my goodness!"

A doll! Made of one piece of wood, painted red. The roughly shaped head had no hair, and the bottom part had a bell-shaped skirt. A string belted its waist, and attached to it dangled a piece of paper. Blanca opened it and found something written in Aita's hand: *ZORIONAK*, Blanca! HAPPY BIRTHDAY.

Blanca clapped her hands. She had forgotten about her birthday in all the excitement about the Blessed Mother.

"Hello." Blanca held up the doll. "My name is Blanca. Who might you be?" The rays of the sun made the paint shimmer like the petals of her mother's roses.

"Rosa!" Blanca hugged the doll. "That will be your name. We're going to be such good friends! I have so much to tell you!"

The son of Don Clemente Itcea y Goyenetche of the great city of Bilbao, Father Xavier Itcea, had been sent to these *menditarrik*, "mountain people," to serve as their rector. He doubted they had the capacity to learn the most rudimentary of subjects, much less appreciate his expertise in Mariology, an expertise he'd developed and honed in his forty years as a Jesuit. He prayed on his black obsidian gemstone rosary, the one he had blessed at Lourdes, for the forbearance he'd need to minister to these people.

Yet he took it as a sign that the bishop held him in high regard that his commission in Indartze began in time for him to celebrate one of his favorite feasts of the Virgin Mary. He stood at the pulpit, eager to enlighten his new parishioners.

"*Eseri mesedez*—please sit down," he said, feeling a rising irritation when the congregation ignored his invitation. Then he remembered the equivalent in their backward dialect: "*Jar zizte.*"

"Today we celebrate the Feast of the Presentation of Mary," Father Itcea began after the squeaking of the pews subsided. "This little-known feast commemorates . . ." he began, then paused to find a simpler word. "This feast celebrates the day Mary's parents, Joachim and Anna, presented the three-year-old Mary to the temple in Jerusalem. To fulfill their promise to God when Anna, after years of being barren, was finally blessed with a child."

In the pews, young mothers smiled at their children, and Father Itcea knew he'd hit the right note for his first homily at Our Lady of Sorrows. For these women would feel sorrowful indeed if they had not been able to fulfill God's purpose for them "to be fruitful and multiply."

He pushed up his round-rimmed eyeglasses and returned to his notes. "When the angel Gabriel came to Mary and asked her to become the mother of the Savior, she had free will to accept or reject his offer. Though only thirteen or fourteen years of age, she had the courage to say, 'Let it be done to me according to your will.'"

The elderly women occupying the first pew assented.

"By saying yes to God, by accepting her destiny"—Father Itcea felt the Holy Spirit speaking through him—"Mary herself became a greater temple than any church or chapel made by man."

Mostly older women and young families attended this early morning Mass. Their faces and hands scrubbed clean, they wore their Sunday best. Handkerchiefs peeking out of their coat pockets, the men held their berets in hands coarsened by work in the fields. The black dresses and hair pulled back into tight buns under mantillas of the older women contrasted with the shorter, waved hair of the younger women, who wore the newer style wide-brimmed felt hats. Their gloved hands held rosaries or decorated silk fans. Most congregants wore religious medallions on gold chains around their necks.

"For each of us, God has a destiny," Father Itcea said. "It is our duty to accept our fate without complaint and without fear. Mary said yes to the Lord even though she was afraid, even though she was just a young, humble virgin. She could not have known that by saying yes she would bring into the world Christ Our Savior, who died for our sins."

Nods from the parishioners and vigorous whispers of concurrence.

"Woe betide those who refuse the will of the Lord who are too fearful to do what God asks of them." Father Itcea felt inspired. "To reject the destiny God has chosen for us is worse than Original Sin: it is our particular sin."

As Father Itcea let his words sink in, he glanced at the stained-glass windows dotting the walls of the church. Most had too much soot on them for him to discern their subject; he'd have to do something about that. One clearly depicted St. Hildegard of Bingen, the nun-mystic from medieval times. Cradling a book on her left knee, she held a stylus in her right hand. The sun shone through the fingers of flame shooting out from St. Hildegard's closed eyes, illuminating a wide-eyed girl in the congregation. Father Itcea hadn't noticed her before. A red ribbon sat atop her fine black hair, cropped close to her round face. She raised her rosary to her lips to kiss. Seemingly just another innocent young girl, she appeared simple in her piety.

Yet something else emanated from her—an aura he had felt on only a few occasions. Perturbed, Father Itcea forgot the final blessing, and then he missed a step on his way down from the pulpit. He realized where he had last felt such spiritual energy: at the sanctuary in Lourdes where the Virgin Mary had appeared to Bernadette of Soubirous almost a century before.

As Blanca dried the dinner plates, her mother sat on the three-legged wooden stool and made a fire on the compacted clay floor against the kitchen's north wall. Blanca hurriedly took her own seat on the small wicker chair her father had made her. She loved this hour, when Ama would tell her a story, one of the same stories Amatxi Angeline had told Ama when she was a little girl.

"Once upon a time," Ama said, her voice bright, "there was a pretty young shepherd girl."

One of Blanca's favorite stories.

"One day when she went up the mountain," Ama continued in a more ominous tone, "a great, frightening storm came down upon the girl. She raced home in fear, abandoning the sheep in the hills. Her mother, on seeing her return home without her flock, shouted at her, 'What do you think you're doing, silly girl? What have you done with the sheep?'"

Ama's now-angry tone sounded all too familiar.

"'They're on the mountain, Ama,' the frightened girl answered. She began to cry.

"'On the mountain? Is that how you look after our property?' The mother yelled, raising her hand to strike her daughter's face. 'You are such a foolish girl! You are useless! May a thousand devils take you!'

"No sooner did she say that, without time even for the mother's hand to strike, when they heard a deafening noise like thunder. As if a thousand bolts of lightning had hit the front door all at once, the ground began to tremble, and it grew dark. A black cloud covered the sky."

Ama poked the fire to make it crackle and then whispered the next part.

"A few minutes later, when everything returned to normal, the shepherd girl was gone."

Ama's eyes widened and her mouth fell open, as if expressing the shock she'd feel if her own daughter disappeared as suddenly.

"A few days later, a shepherd searching for a ram lost on the mountain found his way into a cave. And to his surprise, inside he found not just the lost animal but a young girl sitting astride it. It was the poor shepherd girl who had vanished!"

Blanca squeezed Ama's hand; she squeezed back.

"The shepherd rubbed and rubbed his eyes in case he was dreaming. 'What are you doing alone in such a dark place as this?'

"'I am the devil's prisoner on account of my mother's curse.'

"'Come along with me. I am certain your mother will forgive you.' The shepherd offered her his hand.

"'I cannot leave here unless it is with my mother.'

"To the shepherd's astonishment, no sooner had the girl spoken these words than she disappeared into the depths of the cave. He searched everywhere for her in vain. She was nowhere to be found, so he took his ram and left the cave. He ran down the mountain and went to see the girl's mother to tell her what had happened. But the mother never went up the mountain to find her daughter, and the shepherd girl was never seen again in the town."

Blanca's throat always caught at these words.
Ama's voice livened up as she told the last passage.

"The years passed and the young girl in the cave grew into a beautiful woman, occasionally glimpsed by the people of the village. The country folk around there call her the Lady of Anboto.

"And if that is true, may it go into a pumpkin."
Ama patted Blanca's hand. Telling stories seemed to make Ama so happy. Maybe this was what the Blessed Mother was talking about?

Ama lit a candle from the dying embers.
   "Can you tell me another?" Blanca asked.

Ama's eyes lit up brighter than than full moon streaming in. "I suppose we have time for one more." She tousled Blanca's hair.

"There once lived two sisters. One of them was a witch . . ."

"*Purra, purra,*" called out Blanca. "Here, chick-chick-chick." Moving slowly through the coop, she spread the grain evenly among the rooster and hens. They pecked at each other over the food anyway. "Stop that!" She swatted the rooster as it scratched at her feet. "There's enough for everyone!"

But there wasn't. Blanca picked up the rooster, *Gorritxo*—Little Red—and petted its golden-brown feathers. "I'm sorry I got mad. I know you're hungry."

She let Gorritxo go and took out the jar of sour milk from her apron pocket. She looked for the hen with the black feathers speckled with white. The hen hadn't laid an egg for a while.

"*Purra, purra,*" called out Blanca again as she tapped the jar with her pocket-knife. "Here, chick-chick-chick . . ."

The hen scampered toward her, looking at her with one eye and at the jar with the other. Blanca gave the hen a gentle squeeze, set her down, and poured the soured milk into the bowl set aside for her.

"*Gaixoa*—you poor thing," Blanca waited until the hen had its fill, picked it up and petted it, then took it outside.

She gave the hen a peck and a squeeze. "*Barka nazan!* Forgive me!"

Then she snapped its neck.

The bells of Our Lady of Sorrows tolled twelve, and Father Itcea made his way across the plaza to Bar Herria, Indartze's gathering place. He would enjoy an aperitif and taste the village's appetizers, or *pintxos*. Likely some parishioners would be there, but in every village he'd served, they'd had enough respect for his position to leave him in peace.

The priest grinned as he noticed the small statue of Our Lady of Sorrows in a niche in the wall beside the bar door. A ladybug—a *Katalingorri*—landed on the icon briefly. He took this as an auspicious sign of all the good he could do in this village.

The fiddle music and loud singing greeting him when he opened the door soured his mood.

Soldados, la patria	Soldiers, the homeland
Nos llama a la lid	Calls us to the fight
Juremos por ella	Let us swear for her sake
Vencer o morir	To triumph or to die

The "Himno de Riego," the anthem of anti-monarchists. Father Itcea had heard of radical forces mobilizing against Alfonso XIII. He didn't think they'd reach such a small village so soon.

El mundo vio nunca	The world never saw
Más noble osadía	More noble daring
Ni vio nunca	Nor any day
Más grande el valor	Was greater valor shown
Que aquél, inflamados	Than that, inflamed,
Nos vimos del fuego	We showed at the fire
Excitar a Riego	To awaken in Riego
De patria el amor	The love of his homeland

Men in navy blue berets raised glasses of beer, swaying shoulder to shoulder at the bar and at the tables. The man tending bar ignored him, but Father Itcea refused to call more attention to himself. Priests should be acknowledged immediately upon entering any room. Tightening his jaw, he straightened his cassock and collar and walked over to the group causing all the commotion.

At the table sat a fiddler who looked like a gypsy. Over his lanky frame hung a worn suit. Long, wavy, reddish hair fell about his shoulders, and his tattered straw hat sat on his weathered fiddle case on the floor beside him. A Gaulois hung from his lips, but upon seeing Father Itcea, he put it in an ash tray and extended his hand.

"*Buenos días, Padre,*" the musician said, in accented Castilian. "Good day, Father. My name is William. Can I buy you a drink?"

I enjoy the look on the priest's face when, despite my disheveled appearance, I speak Castilian competently. The proprietor of the house, Old Simon, hastens over. A thickset man of indeterminate mature age, he is above average height, with skin leathered by the sun and a great shock of untidy black hair escaping in a bushy mass from under his beret, or what the locals called a *boneta*. My drinking and singing companions slink away.

Balanced on Old Simon's tray sit a carafe of the house red wine and a bottle of cognac. He pours me a glass of the wine, then greets the priest in Basque before switching to Castilian.

"It's Domecq cognac, special for you, Father Itcea," Old Simon says. "The regular stuff befits only muleteers, not an esteemed man of the cloth such as yourself."

"Thank you," Father Itcea says frostily.

I hope Old Simon goes away soon but know from my two weeks here he will not.

"We are honored that a priest of your stature would come to serve our humble parish," Old Simon continues.

"I hope to follow in the footsteps of my order's founder, Saint Ignatius of Loiola"—the priest tastes the cognac—"and serve wherever the Lord summons me."

"I visited Loiola." I seize the opening. "I love the cathedral—"

"—My wife tells me you give a beautiful homily," Old Simon interrupts. "She attends Mass daily. I would join her myself on Sundays if I could move about more easily." He pats his left leg. "I almost lost this in ninety-eight."

The door opens and a group of young men in work clothes take up their places at the bar, as they have every day at this hour. I'm happy to see my new acquaintance, Cruz, among them. The young man has been one of my best sources for village goings on, and he seems to appreciate the opportunity our conversations provide him to improve his Castilian.

Old Simon turns to acknowledge them, then back to us. "*Algo más?* Anything else?"

I'm glad the priest declines another cognac. It's the most expensive liquor here.

"We'll let you know when we're ready for more."

I am eager to move Old Simon along. He makes his way to the bar, with a slight limp I haven't noticed before.

"He's very . . . friendly." I lift my glass of house red wine to Father Itcea.

"Yes." The priest raises his glass and brow simultaneously and sips his cognac. "Too familiar. He reminds me of the servants we had at home; they didn't know their place."

I take the hint.

"Tell me, William," he says. "What brings you to this small village?"

I explain that I'm following in the tradition of itinerant musicians, that I go from village to village with my fiddle, collecting songs and friends along the way. I don't tell him all the reasons I have come here.

"That song you just played," he says. "Where did you learn it?"

I tell him I'd learned it in a bar in Madrid, but I do not share my interest in its political significance.

"You presumably don't realize, as an outsider," he says, "that that song is the rallying cry of rebels." He lowers his voice, as priests do when giving penance in a confessional. "Perhaps it would be wise not to play that particular song in Indartze."

The young men do shots of whiskey at the bar.

"The people here are calm and contented. As a fellow Basque, I can tell you most of them function best when guided by the principles of their pope and their king." His tone sharpens. "The provisional superior sent me here because my predecessor did not provide the people of this village with such guidance."

He stands and tosses a few coins onto the table. "These drinks are on me."

"You are so kind." I force a smile to my lips, though I know he means to dismiss me.

When the tavern door closes behind him, I count the coins. Enough for our drinks, with plenty left over. I open my fiddle case and look through my sheet music, then make some notes of the conversation to flesh out later, per my nightly schedule. I decide to play a song my long-lost sweetheart had taught me many years ago. It's about four women having a grand time drinking and joking as they play the local card game *mus*. I don't know all the words, but think I can get by on the first verse. That should be invitation enough for others to join in. I improvise an introduction on my fiddle, then sing along to the melody.

Herriko besta biharmunean	The day after the village festival
Berek dakiten txoko batean	In a corner they know well
Lau andre, hiru mutxurdin	Four women: three spinsters
Bat alarguna, jarriak itzalean	And one widow
Harri xabal baten gainean	Sit at a wide stone
Ari dira trukean	Gambling

As I hoped, the men who abandoned me at the priest's arrival return, as do young men from the bar. They sing better than I do and with better pronunciation, though none of them critize mine, so I am happy to follow their lead.

They know more verses than I remember, and I make a mental note to find out what they mean. I recognize the final verse and join my voice to theirs.

Besta bigarren egunberean	On the second day of the festival
Lau gatu xahar anjelusean	When the angelus rings, four cats
Bat mainguz hiru saltoka	One lame, three jumping
Sorginak, pujes!	They are witches, off with you!
Zoatzila bidean	Going down the road
Ikusi ditut amets batean	I saw it in a dream
Akelarre gainean	About the witches' coven

When I first heard this song, I loved the twist at the end. Until I learned the dark history of the witch persecutions that happened here in the seventeenth century.

Birdsong outside her window awakened Blanca.

"Listen, Rosa!" She shook awake her doll. "The birds are welcoming us to a new day."

Quickly changing from her bedclothes to her work dress, Blanca put Rosa into the apron of her skirt and went outside. Even before she had her *kafesnea*, her coffee-with-milk, Blanca made sure the chickens got their breakfast. As she walked to the henhouse, she saw Cruz coming down the path. Blanca quickened her pace when she saw what her brother held in his arms.

"A kitty!" she told Rosa.

Cruz held it as he would a baby. He stroked the kitten's little head, and it purred and purred.

"I found her on Aranzibia Hill." Cruz laid the kitten in Blanca's arms. "All by herself. No mother around. She's old enough to be weaned, though it looks as if she's injured." He pointed to the hind left leg. "You have ten years now. I think you can look after her well enough." He put his arm around Blanca and smiled. "What do you think?"

"*Baietz*," Blanca said. "Yes, indeed!"

The kitty looked up at her and meowed softly, reaching its front paw out to her. Blanca's heart melted.

"I'll call her *Xuriko*—the white one." She held the kitty close.

"Pure and white, like you," Cruz said.

Blanca hugged her brother, careful not to squish Rosa or the kitty. It felt so good to be surrounded by such love.

CHAPTER THREE

For the first time since he'd been installed at Indartze, Father Itcea could spend Monday, his day off, as he pleased. While not nearly as cosmopolitan as Bilbao, St. Jean Pied de Port had a brisker pace than Indartze. He enjoyed the bustle of the crowds. Peasant women and city folk came here on market day to buy fresh fruit, Iraty cheese made of sheep's milk, or the *piquello* chilis so difficult to find these days in Spain. The priest also enjoyed the chance to have an aperitif away from the accusatory looks of his parishioners.

He didn't bother with Basque here, even though they spoke the elegant dialect used in the *Linguae Vasconum Primitiae*, penned by the sixteenth-century priest Bernard Etxepare. Indeed, Father Itcea reveled in the opportunity to practice the French he'd studied for so many years in preparation for an evangelizing mission to francophone Africa that never materialized.

He walked into Café Ttipia on the Place Floquet and sat at his usual table facing the window. Before he had a chance to catch his attention, the waiter Gabriel approached with a *café noisette* and a glass of brandy.

"Good afternoon, *monsieur*," Gabriel said. "Good to see you again."

"You as well, Gabriel," Father Itcea said. "It has taken me longer than I anticipated to orient myself to my new parish."

"*Ah, bon!*" exclaimed Gabriel. "I congratulate you. You received the position to the cathedral you hoped for?"

"Alas, no." The priest tamped down his bitterness. "My superiors deemed it would better serve the Lord if I put my expertise in Mariology and local languages into service at the more humble parish of Our Lady of Sorrows in Indartze." He tasted the brandy and waved aside the sugar Gabriel offered.

"No doubt you will serve the people there well. Would you care for anything else?"

The reminder of his lowly post had spoiled Father Itcea's appetite. "Do you have a copy of *Le Monde*?"

"*Bien sur*—of course." Gabriel went to the bar and returned with a newspaper tucked under his arm. "I apologize, Father; another patron must have it. I do have the Saturday edition of *Le Matin*."

"That will have to do," Father Itcea said. Though not as comprehensive as *Le Monde*, *Le Matin* featured one of his favorite foreign correspondents, G.U. He didn't have to look far to find him.

December 13, 1930
REVOLT STARTS IN SPAIN: REBELS TAKE BORDER CITY OF JACA—by G.U.

Precisely the city where he'd hoped to serve! Father Itcea cursed under his breath and read on:

The garrison at Jaca, in the Pyrenees near the French border, has revolted and imprisoned its officers in the fort. For some time, Spanish republicans have insisted that when the time came they would move against the monarchy.

"*Ave Maria!*" Father Itcea grasped his gold Miraculous Medallion pendant. *Spare us the evils of revolution!*

The Jaca uprising was fomented by alien and radical military and civilian elements, but sufficient troops have now been concentrated south and west of Jaca and Huesca to defeat the rebels against the Crown in short order.

The priest exhaled the breath he didn't know he was holding.

Serious unrest, with repeated disorders in larger cities, has been prevalent in Spain for the last month. On November 15, a general strike, accompanied by serious rioting, gripped Madrid and rapidly spread from the Spanish capital to other cities. Business and industry were crippled by these strikes, and more than 20,000,000 people were directly affected.

Twenty million people! Father Itcea shook his head. Would these rabble-rousers ever learn? Why did they think they could run the country's affairs better than the king? Left to their own devices, they fought among themselves and took what belonged to others.

Still, he wondered why he'd heard nothing about this rebellion against the monarchy; it had happened two days ago.

In the capital and other cities, the police began a quiet round-up of agitators. To quell the unrest, the government imposed martial law.

Ah. Father Itcea took a last swig of his brandy. Martial law would include censorship of the press. Perhaps Providence had a plan for him after all. If he had been sent to Jaca, he would have arrived too late to foil the rebellion. In Indartze, he could still save his parishioners from themselves, though he couldn't protect his parishioners from potential threats of which he himself was unaware.

He snapped his fingers at Gabriel, a plan formulating in his mind.

The sweet smell of the pastries at Malkorra made Blanca's mouth water. Everyone seemed to have come here as soon as Mass let out. Ama had given Blanca money to buy bread. It would taste so good with the cheese her mother had made with sheep's milk.

She was the only child here by herself, so the grown-ups talked over her.

"Well, I hear she was seen driving around with a young man in that new automobile of his," said a woman behind her in line. "At night."

"Hmm," her companion said. "You know what that means."

The two women cackled like hens.

"I tell you, there's no way he could afford that new tractor," another woman said. "He must be smuggling on the side."

"No shame in that," a man's voice said. "They've got to eat. With these prices, I would do it again myself if I could."

Blanca recalled what her father had said about smuggling. "It's illegal, but not a sin." The things smugglers carried didn't hurt anybody. They just dealt in hard-to-get items like sugar, coffee, and lace.

Then Blanca overheard people saying something about an election coming up, something she didn't understand. Anyway, the pastries in the display case held her attention: *gateau basque, urrakin egiña* chocolates, *brazo gitano* cream-filled puffs, toasted almond cakes called *Jesuítas.*

She put her coins on the counter. "Two baguettes, please."

The salesgirl whispered to Blanca, "I'm afraid that's not enough even for one."

Blanca's cheeks warmed.

"You're Cruz's sister, aren't you?" The salesgirl said. "Is he around to bring the rest? I'll save your place in line."

"Uh . . . he should be here soon." Blanca bit her lip.

A young woman left her coffee and *El Pueblo* newspaper at her table and approached. Her straw-colored hair flowed to her shoulders and her eyes shone the color of cornflowers.

"I'll take care of it." The woman put her arm around Blanca. "And with the change, why not a treat?" Her smile was as radiant as the Blessed Mother's. "What would you like, sweetheart?"

Blanca could not believe this beautiful stranger's kindness.

The door chimes rang.

"She likes white bonbons the most," Cruz's voice called out, matter-of-fact. He stood beside Blanca now, holding a bag of groceries.

He turned toward the stranger. "I appreciate your generosity. I have enough." His face flushed. "For the bread."

He handed coins to the salesgirl, who gave two baguettes to Blanca. Cruz took Blanca's hand and walked her to the door. She turned around to wave goodbye to the beautiful girl, but she and Cruz had locked eyes. They appeared to see only each other.

The train carrying Blanca and her mother whistled as it pulled into the station. Amatxi Angeline felt ill, and Ama thought a visit might cheer her up. Blanca gripped her mother's hand through fancy silk gloves, the ones the girl wore for special occasions. The coat smelled of mothballs, and the wool made her itch, but Blanca wanted to look nice for her grandmother.

"*Hemen dun*—here's our stop," her mother said.

Blanca did her best to keep up with her mother's long gait without scuffing her patent leather shoes, yet Ama didn't seem concerned about tidiness for once. Blanca held tight to her rosary in her pocket and prayed to the Blessed Mother that Amatxi would get well.

Young couples in suits and dresses dallied alongside single men moving briskly, holding well-worn briefcases or battered suitcases. Pairs of women chatted, arms linked, their eyes dancing under smart hats made of straw, banded with ribbons.

"*Harat*," her mother said. "Over there. By that sign. That's where Maria Jesus will meet us." Maria Jesus lived next door to Amatxi Angeline.

The sign said *Pèlerinage à Lourdes*. Next to it on a pole hung a kind of priest's vestment, a gold cross embroidered on a big piece of white cloth. And that's where the queue began, with stretchers of the sick and dying lined up for the pilgrimage to Lourdes. The first stretcher, supported by two men in suits and fedoras, held a woman who looked as if only in her twenties. All skin and bones, she appeared close to death. Her skin appeared sallow against the dark fabric of her dress. Behind her an older man about Blanca's father's age sat in a special high-backed wooden chair with wheels attached to the sides.

A tall, thin man in monk's robes stood facing the pilgrims, his finger to his lips.

"Silence!" His reedy voice cut through the din. "We must show respect to Our Lady!"

"Blanca." Ama nudged her forward. "Let's move out of their way."

Blanca did as she was told, though she couldn't keep her eyes off the pilgrims. So many people—young and old—in wheelchairs, on stretchers, walking with canes. All with such hope in their eyes that the holy waters from the grotto would heal them.

A young man in messy clothes broke from the line of pilgrims, rushed toward Blanca, and fell to his knees before her. He kept looking at her face as his arms and legs jerked wildly.

"*Gaizkatu ene gaitza!* Rid me of my illness!" He reached for Blanca's hand. In a protective stance, Ama moved to face him and held Blanca tightly behind her.

"Keep your hands off my daughter!" warned Ama.

And though Blanca could not see her mother's face, she knew from her tone that her eyes blazed. Policemen approached and took the man away. Blanca could focus only on what he'd said. *Gaizkatu* was the exact word the Blessed Mother had used. Blanca didn't know it meant "to heal."

Blanca beamed as she took her mother's hand as they exited the station. What a good mission for the Blessed Mother to give her. She hoped she'd be worthy of it.

CHAPTER FOUR

7 eanáir, 1931
January 7, 1931

My fiddle case in hand, I walk down the stairs from my ramshackle room above Bar Herria, the only place offering rooms cheap enough for my extended stay here. I take a drag on my Gaulois and ponder the Basque songs I've learned so far. Songs bear the knowledge of the ordinary people whose experiences interest me most.

Music had drawn me and Caireann to each other all those years ago, and memories of our doomed courtship still haunt me when I play. She had the gift for singing that brought her brethren praise but girls reproach if shared in public. Thus all the sweeter were the private moments we spent, just us two: she, singing the songs of anguish, the specialty of her people; and I, plucking at my fiddle until I found the perfect harmony.

My eyes adjust to the dim lamplight as I enter the dining room, and I find the corner table where I usually eat. It sits empty, as do the surrounding tables. The old polished wood gleams, and the sour scents of beer and the sweet smell of *patxaran*, a local liqueur made from sloe fruits, battle for ascendency. Old Simon approaches me immediately.

"Good afternoon, *señor*," he says. His tray holds a basket of sourdough bread and a decanter of red wine. He removes the stopper and pours me a glass. "*Menú del día?*"

"*Como de costumbre*—as usual." I don't bother asking what the "menu of the day" is. Regardless, I will eat it: it will be hearty, delicious, and inexpensive.

Old Simon returns to the bar. I taste the wine and place my box of cigarettes on the table. I open my fiddle case and retrieve the collection of verses I bought at Indartze's bookshop, after posting mail to my editor. One song, written by Sabine Elizalde, has caught my attention for the few words I recognize: *Indartze* (the name of this town), *Maria*, and *saindu* (an obvious calque of the Latin *sanctus*).

I count the beats per line; it has the 10/8 meter typical of Basque song. I find a tune on my fiddle that goes to rhythm, following along with the words in my head:

Jende onak, huna gu huna gu	Good people, we come
Kantatu nahi dinagu	To sing this song
Egi zuzena beti aitortu	To tell the truth
Saindu Mairaren kondu	About Saint Maria

I sing the next verse quietly to myself.

Indartzen sortu eta hazia	Born and raised in Indartze
Indartsu zaiku Maria	Maria grew strong
Neska on ona, zoragarria	A good and wonderful girl
Bedeinkatzen gaituena	She blesses us

How frustrating not to understand what it means.

Old Simon approaches with a steaming tureen of chicken broth. "Here you are," he says. "Can I get you anything else?"

I glance behind him to the still-empty dining room. "There is something you can help me with." I point to the songbook. "Do you have a moment to join me for a glass?"

"*Con mucho gusto, señor.*" Old Simon takes a glass from an adjacent table and sits beside me.

"I may have to get us a second bottle," I say.

"*Salut!*" He takes a drink and puts his glass down beside the song sheets. "I know this song." He reads silently. "I used to sing it during Lent when I was boy. We would go around from farm to farm singing this and other saint songs, banging canes to the tempo, until the woman of the house gave us something to eat." He smiles at the memory.

"It's about a saint?" I say.

The tavern door opens. Old Simon glances at the wavy-haired boy who enters and motions for him to take a seat at the bar.

"He can wait," he says, gruffly. "He only wants a coffee, anyway." Old Simon reads two verses under his breath. "The first part tells about a girl named Maria Gurrutxetegia from Indartze whose example blesses us. We must not have sung the whole thing way back when." He points to the third verse. "Things get interesting here." He sings, stopping every other verse to translate.

Zigorren maltzukeriak	Zigor's trickery
Egin gaitu tranpatu	Fooled us
Erran-marranak sustatu	Provoked false rumors
Sualdia kausitu	Caused a conflagration
Bilogorri hori hil zuten	They killed that red-head
Sorgina zela zioten	Saying she was a witch
Zigortzeko hartu ordezkoa	In her stead, they punished
Gure gaixoa Maria	Our poor Maria

"Do you mind?" I take my notebook and pen from my fiddle case. "I love learning about songs in the local language."

He waves his hand in assent and continues with his singing.

Zehatu ukabilka	They shattered her with blows
Odola burrustaka	Blood dripping, head to toe
Halare egon da azkarra	She stayed strong
Gure saindu Maria	Our sainted Maria
Zigorrek Maria salatu:	Zigor accused Maria
"Oihu egin zan—haiz sorgina"	"Cry it out—you are a witch!"
"Gezurra duk hori:gaiztegina!"	"That's a lie, evildoer!"
Bihotz garbi duenak	Said the pure-hearted one

What horrific torture this girl endured! How disturbing that children sang this while begging for treats!

"This verse I do remember," Old Simon says. "The priest told us to slow down here, to emphasize its message about God's salvation." He sings slowly, the words weighing on his lips.

Sumetan kantatzen salmoa	At the pyre, a psalm
Gure Maria saindua	Our sainted Maria sang
Zerurat igan da: Gloria!	She went to heaven: Gloria!
Betikotz gozatzera	To enjoy it forever

His eyes tear up. "We used to harmonize that last 'Gloria' in two voices. It still moves me to think about how beautiful it sounded."

"I can well imagine it: innocent children singing sweetly in harmony." I pour us each more wine.

"I've never sung the words as an adult, or read them on paper," Old Simon says. "We would memorize whatever the priest taught us. I can see now why he left these verses out."

"Indeed. Do you know any more about the girl? Was she a witch? Or a saint?" I believe in neither but have learned to keep my opinions to myself.

"Bah! Who knows?" Old Simon shrugs. "The priest believed she should have been made a saint. He told us her ashes or relics were hidden somewhere, that right after Maria's death people prayed on them and were cured of illness and deformities. He spent his whole life looking for them."

He stands up, picking up the tureen full of now-cold soup. A plate of roasted chicken and potatoes awaits me on the counter.

"Some say he lost his mind in the end," Old Simon says. "Others say he needed more time."

"Who do you think is right?" I ask.

"Who am I to say? Each side has its points. Though I served as that priest's altar boy, and I remember him hunting around Our Lady of Sorrows for something." He smirks mischievously. "And that church holds many secrets."

"Here you go, my dear." Amatxi Angeline poured steaming milk over the coffee and Blanca smiled at her grandmother, eyeing the little cubes of sugar in the ceramic bowl on the embroidered doily. She wondered if it would be polite to take one before her grandmother offered. Her mother's severe look gave the answer.

Amatxi Angeline picked up two cubes, dropping one into Blanca's cup and another into her own.

"*Azukre bi, gu biok ezti!*" The words slipped from Blanca's lips. "Two sugars make us both sweet!"

This drew a chuckle even from Blanca's mother. They used to say this all the time, when they could still afford sugar. Blanca waited until her grandmother and mother drank from their cups before tasting her own. The sugary *kafesnea* scalded her tongue though it tasted delicious. Waiting to be invited to speak, Blanca tried to sit still and pay attention. The conversation began with the usual catching up about people she didn't know.

"You remember Miguelito from *Ariztea borda*?" Her grandmother asked. "Or should I say Miguel from Ariztea House. He is twenty-five now. He's not the little boy he was when you left ..."

As Amatxi talked, Blanca stirred her coffee with the little silver spoon with the ornate handle, slowly so that it didn't clank against the cup. Between sips, she surveyed her grandmother's kitchen. Amatxi always seemed to get something new between visits. Blanca looked at the delicate lace curtain moving to and fro as the gentle breeze wafted in, the wooden humpback-shaped clock sitting on the mantel between brightly covered ceramic pots. The stoneware gourd with flammée glaze, a gold and rose-cut diamond snuffbox with an MR monogram. Nothing new here. She'd make an excuse soon so that she could explore. For now, Blanca looked at her grandmother and tried to seem interested.

". . . they say he's looking for a wife," Amatxi was saying. "And I myself saw him walking a young lady home after the shops closed last Monday evening."

Ama clenched her jaw. "Well, that doesn't necessarily mean anything. Maybe she felt afraid to walk home by herself in the dark."

"Not this girl," Amatxi said. "She's younger than Miguel in years but older in other ways." Her brown eyes sparkled. "Oh my, where are my manners?" She shuffled to the cupboard and took down a rectangular tray covered with white tissue paper, then placed it on the table. Blanca knew only one word on the golden ribbon wrapping the tissue paper, but it made her mouth water: *pâtisserie*—bakery.

"Ama, you shouldn't have," Blanca's mother said. "I told you, we ate at the station."

"*Ba*," Amatxi waved the comment away. "That food is no good. Nothing like this." She placed three dessert plates on the table. The fancy china plates, with blue birds painted on them. "Nothing's too good for my favorite granddaughter."

Blanca loved it when Amatxi said this, even though she was the only granddaughter.

As her grandmother untied the fancy ribbon, Blanca pressed her hands against her tummy so Amatxi would not hear the growling. She and her mother hadn't eaten anything since their potato soup and bread last night.

Amatxi folded the tissue paper neatly, not a tear in it, and set it next to Blanca so that she could take it home. Then with a twirl of one hand, she offered the tray with the other.

"Blanca, which one would you like?"

"Anything would be fine." Blanca remembered her mother's advice to take graciously whatever Amatxi offered. She knew she would not be disappointed. Before her sat a tray full of white chocolate bonbons.

"Oh, *mila esker*, Amatxi!" Blanca beamed. "Thanks so much!" Half a dozen candies, two for each of them!

Blanca took her time eating the first one, knowing she wouldn't get any candies at home. The powdery sweetness melted on her tongue. She half-listened to the conversation. Ama told Amatxi Angeline about the pilgrims at the train station.

"And then this crazy man came up to Blanca and threw himself at her feet, begging her to cure him. He frightened us," Ama said. "Now that I think of it, how silly for him to believe a little girl like Blanca could help him."

Of course she's right, Blanca thought. The bonbon lost its sweetness.

"Well, I don't know about that." Amatxi looked deeply into Blanca's eyes, then furrowed her brow. "Bernadette Soubirous was a young girl too."

"Ama," Blanca's mother said, "I don't think this is the time—"

"—It's the perfect time." Grandmother Angeline squeezed Blanca's hand. "Blanca's old enough now. I can tell she's ready to hear about how Our Lady cured me of my *erormina*, the falling sickness."

Amatxi gestured toward the oak chest in the corner. Blanca loved the engraving on it: *Hemen sartzen dena bere etxean da*. The one who enters here is home.

"Could you get it for me please, Maider?"

Frowning, Ama obeyed her mother. She pulled an object from the trunk and placed it on the table. Then she went to the kitchen and returned with a tonic.

"It's a toy train!" Blanca exclaimed. About the size of a large brick, it was just right for Rosa to ride on. She wished Ama had let her bring her doll, so that she could try it out.

"Oh, it's more than that." Amatxi's eyes sparkled. "Take a closer look."

Blanca noticed the train's engine and caboose were made of white porcelain. "The chimney has '1858' written on it, and 'Lourdes' on the side," Blanca said. The lettering was in gold. The wagon-cart and wheels were gold-plated, too.

Too fancy to be a toy.

"That's not all. Look!" Amatxi lifted the lids off the chimney and the caboose.

"A carafe and sugar tin!" Blanca exclaimed.

"Yes, I thought it odd when I first saw it, that an object made to honor Our Lady of Lourdes could also be so practical," Amatxi said. "Yet something inside me told me to buy it, and it was a good thing I did."

She touched the porcelain lovingly.

"I would use this set to serve guests who wanted to hear about the miracle that cured me. I pray the Rosary every day in gratitude to Our Lady of Lourdes for healing me," Amatxi said. "When I was little, I had two or three seizures a day. Some so severe I fell unconscious. My father was not a religious man, but he grew desperate when I had a particularly severe convulsion when he was conducting business near Lourdes. Spasms shook my whole body and blood flowed from my mouth. Pilgrims to the holy shrine insisted on taking me to the sacred spring. They helped my father lift me into the water three times, pleading with Our Lady to heal me."

Blanca held her second bonbon midair, fascinated by the story. She put the chocolate on the dessert plate, wiped her fingers on the linen napkin, and put her hands in her lap.

"I never suffered a seizure again." Angeline looked up and closed her eyes. "The doctors could find no medical explanation for my recovery. It was a miracle!"

"A miracle!" echoed Blanca.

Ama went back to the trunk and came back with a bottle shaped in the image of the Virgin Mary. "People come from all over for this holy water," she said. "Your grandmother gives it away for free. But as you can see," she made a gesture encompassing the whole room, "many of them find ways to express their gratitude."

"This bottle of holy water is for you, Blanca," Amatxi said. "Use it well."

Blanca took the bottle into her hands as solemnly as she took the Eucharist at Communion. She knew exactly what she would do with it.

I fumble my way upstairs, one hand gripping my glass of whiskey, the other turning my room key. The final song brought me back to the last time I saw Caireann. The tune is seared in my memory as her favorite, despite its tale of unrequited love. I know I cannot tamp down the feelings about to overwhelm me; heartbreak cleaves my chest as if we'd just parted. I'm embarrassed the ache is so raw even after twenty years.

I gulp down the rest of my whiskey, unlock my fiddle case, and open the zippered compartment I've fashioned inside. I take out the only photo I have of Caireann, her smile radiant and her cheeks rosy, and put it beside the gift she gave me when we promised ourselves to each other. Too poor at the time to buy her a ring, I'd given her the only valuable object I'd had, a chromed stainless steel and pewter pocket watch engraved with the Celtic Tree of Life.

"I'll return to you before the year is through," I'd whispered to her amid my tears. Tragically, the Great War had other plans.

And Caireann gave me something she swore had belonged to her father, though I was certain she'd purchased it especially for me: a Waterman gold-filigree eyedropper safety pen. Too precious for everyday use, it's used only for the final drafts of my songs and stories. Its leather traveling case feels as soft and supple as the day she gave it to me.

My head throbs and my vision blurs, yet before flopping onto the bed I manage to put the pencase and photo on the little table that doubles as a nightstand and desk. Heartache, regret, and bitterness weigh me down as I fall asleep.

I also used that pen to write Caireann after we'd parted—one unanswered letter after another.

They returned home from Amatxi Angeline's at sunset, in time for Blanca to try out her plan. Holding tight to the bottle of holy water as she approached the front door, Blanca called for her kitty. Ama went inside to prepare dinner.

"*Hator*, Xuriko." Blanca clucked her tongue. "Come here, sweetie."

Xuriko appeared, meowing and rubbing herself against Blanca's legs, shedding her fluffy white fur onto Blanca's skirt. Blanca would be sure to brush that off before Ama could see it.

Xuriko followed her to the side of the house, where Blanca kept her kitty's bowls. Aita had made them out of wood, especially for Xuriko. Blanca would save some of her dinner to put in the food bowl later, but into the empty water bowl she poured the holy water from Lourdes.

Xuriko dipped her muzzle into the water, then just stared at her.

"Aren't you thirsty?" She petted her kitty. "This water is magical. It will make you feel better."

Unmoving, Xuriko looked at her blankly.

"Blanca!" Her mother's voice carried through the kitchen window above. "Time to peel potatoes!"

"Coming, Ama!" Blanca called back.

Xuriko stood there, not drinking.

Blanca dipped her finger into the water bottle, then took Xuriko by the scruff of her neck.

"I don't know if this will work, but it's worth a try." Blanca rubbed Xuriko's injured leg with the holy water.

She kissed Xuriko's neck. "Be sure to drink that water too." She put her kitty down. "The Blessed Mother wants to help us, but we must do our part."

As her kitten finally took a drink, Blanca recited a quick prayer: "And if it works for you, maybe it'll heal Aita too."

Father Itcea returned to Indartze with renewed purpose. Clearly, he had been sent to this backward parish to ensure it did not fall into chaos the way Jaca had. Now he knew why he'd had a lifelong interest in languages and Mariology. His spiritual director had told him that one day these "holy desires" would make their greater purpose known.

That day had finally come.

His realization came to him during morning prayers. Today—the seventh of January—was the birthday of Bernadette Soubirous, the young peasant girl to whom the Virgin Mary appeared in Lourdes in 1858. The Virgin Mary had told Bernadette, "I am the Immaculate Conception," thereby confirming Pope Pius IX's own articulation of this belief four years earlier. This laid the groundwork for a spiritual awakening among thousands of people.

That kind of religious fervor would inoculate the parishioners of Our Lady of Sorrows against political radicalism. Many Basques felt a special affinity for Bernadette because she hailed from the Occitan region, not far from the French Basque Country. Bernadette had been beatified in 1925, so only the final steps to her canonization remained. A humble peasant girl elevated to sainthood—that would be the perfect model of piety and obedience for the simple people of Indartze.

Father Itcea made a list of what he remembered about Bernadette and her visions:

1. Bernadette was only fourteen years old when the Virgin Mary appeared to her above a rose bush in a grotto. Small and prone to illness caused by an impoverished childhood, Bernadette nonetheless summoned the strength to receive graciously all visitors seeking her intercession with the Virgin Mary.

From his desk drawer, Father Itcea withdrew a photograph of the young Bernadette that he'd purchased on his last pilgrimage. A white scarf covered her hair as modesty dictated, and she wore a serious expression. Her dark eyes looked directly into the camera, bespeaking a quiet confidence unusual in a young girl of her station.

2. The Virgin Mary told Bernadette to return to the grotto every night for two weeks, a period later called *la Quinzaine sacre*, or "the holy fortnight." Though her parents forbade her to continue with these visits, she persisted.

3. The Virgin Mary instructed Bernadette "to drink of the water of the spring, to wash in it, and eat the herb that grew there" as an act of penance. The grotto's muddy waters cleared, and fresh water flowed thereafter.

4. Tens of thousands of pilgrims have subsequently claimed to be cured by bathing in or drinking from this spring.

Even though these events spanned decades, Bernadette had not yet been canonized. The Vatican had strict rules: two miracles had to be attributed to the candidate after his death for consideration, and both had to be verified by ecclesiastical authorities after an arduous examination. Father Itcea had heard a rumor that Bernadette's body had been found intact even though she had died fifty years ago. That could constitute the first miracle.

What if he uncovered a second miracle? New, undisputed claims of Bernadette's intercessions would be difficult to find. He said a quick prayer to the Virgin Mary that she might assist him in his quest.

The thunder clapped louder with each spark from the fireplace. Despite the cold and wet that seemed to seep into her bones no matter how many layers she wore, Blanca felt content. It had been a long time since the whole family had huddled around the fire to eat chestnuts.

And tell stories. Aita's turn tonight. Leaning on Cruz, he took his seat, the wicker chair groaning with him. He winced, then winked at Blanca, but she knew he was in pain.

Yet he brightened when he told stories.

"It seems that a young Basque woman went to take her sheep to pasture one day, when she happened upon the most handsome young man she had ever seen. She could tell right away he was a foreigner. Not only did he have fair skin and grey eyes, peeking from underneath his blond hair were his ears, one bigger than the other."

"*To!* Come now!" Ama said to him. "Not a story about those ugly people!"

Blanca thought the boy sounded beautiful.

Aita continued: "The shepherd girl gets closer to the boy, and she sees that he's crying. 'Why are you so sad?' she asks. And in answer, he sings:

"Atzo nurbait izan düzü ene ait'ametara
    Yesterday someone came to see my mother and father

"Gük alkhar maite dügüla haien abertitzera
    And told them we love each other

"Hürrüntaaztez alkhar ganik fite ditin lehia
    To try to separate us as soon as possible

"Eta eztitian jünta kasta agotarekila
    And that it is forbidden to mix with the *agota* caste"

Blanca didn't know about the *agotas* but didn't want to interrupt. She loved her father's singing. Though his body had weakened, his voice remained strong.

"Agotak badiadila badizüt entzütia:
    That there are *agotas*, I have heard said

"Zük erraiten deitadazüt ni ere banizala
    You tell me that I'm one, too

"Egündano ükhen banü demendren leinhuria
    If I ever had that lowly lineage

"Enündüzün ausartüren begila so'gitera
    I would never have dared to look you in the eye"

Like many other stories about young people in love, this could end either happily or very badly. Blanca listened closely as Aita modulated into the final verse, to see which way this one would go.

"Hori hala balinbada, naietarik etzira
    If it is so, you are among the undesirable

"Ezi zure beharriak alkhar üdüri dira
    For your ears look alike

"Agota denak txipiago badü beharri bata
    All *agotas* have one ear smaller than the other

"*Aitari erranen diot biak bardin tüzüla*
I will tell my father that yours are the same size"

Blanca clapped and repeated the last verse. Ama and Cruz joined in. Just the happy ending she had hoped for. The rain suddenly stopped. Xuriko jumped on the windowsill, her injured leg all better now. Blanca unhooked the shutters and giggled at what she saw there: *hortz ederra!* A beautiful rainbow!

Kneeling in the middle of the grove with the four oak trees, Blanca prayed the Rosary quietly to herself. She had already prayed the five decades of the Joyful Mysteries and was in the middle of the third Luminous Mystery, the "Proclamation of the Kingdom of God." She hoped the Blessed Mother would appear soon, but then she pushed the thought out of her mind. She had no right to make demands of her. In her rush to leave the house, though, Blanca had not eaten any breakfast, and her stomach growled. The sun bore down on her and she started feeling faint.

"Open your eyes, my dear child," a soft voice called out. Blanca beamed that the Blessed Mother called her "dear."

"Ama Maite Maria," Blanca said, "I'm so happy you have appeared to me again!" The Blessed Mother looked different than last time. She had long hair the color of fire, tied behind her neck, and a golden halo framed her head. A Bible rested on her lap.

But her smile was the same, reaching all the way to her eyes. "You have passed the first test, Blanca. You believed in the power of the water from Lourdes and used it to heal Xuriko."

"Yes, Ama!" Blanca cried in happiness.

Blanca kept looking at the vision, letting the deep sense of peace fill her. The gold of the halo twinkled in the sun. Birdsong filled the air, a soft breeze from the north wafted through the leaves, cowbells echoed from the valley below.

She closed her eyes to take in these soothing sounds, so grateful the Blessed Mother had chosen to appear to her in this beautiful place. Then a new sound arose. Blanca opened her eyes and gasped.

The Blessed Mother had disappeared, but beside the biggest oak tree a spring now bubbled.

I sit outside Bar Herria, finishing my *café solo* and smoking my Gaulois. I think over what I've learned about the people and the culture in Indartze—from the conversations I've been able to have in Castilian or French—at the bar, in the handball court, on the street, during card games. As a rule, the Basques work hard and deal fairly with each other when it comes to wages and prices; a man who doesn't fulfill his promises is never trusted again. More practical than political, Basques find ways to carry on with their lives and livelihoods no matter what the political winds may be.

Like their brethren on the French side, the Basques here are taciturn in the public square though quite emotional in the public house. I have seen the eyes of tough men water when recalling lost loved ones, especially their mothers, no matter how long ago they may have passed. I recall the many, many songs dedicated to mothers I've collected since my first trip to the Basque Country twenty years ago. Here in Indartze, I realize, all the songs and goings-on I have collected have come from men.

I have to find a way to talk to the women here, for in every village I've visited, it is the women who have their finger on the pulse of their community. Their accounts lend a verisimilitude to my stories that others lack, or so I've been told.

Old Simon approaches with my bill, then turns his attention to a couple two tables over. I haven't seen them before. They appear to be in their early forties like me. In contrast to my vagabond attire, he wears a coat, tie, and bowler hat; she wears a floral print dress and on her short hair is a cloche with a rolled brim. From Old Simon's litany of questions, I learn the couple have come to Indartze from Barcelona to visit relatives, whom they will meet shortly in Our Lady of Sorrows. They express surprise that a small Basque village would offer a Mass in Castilian.

"Oh, yes." Old Simon takes the basket of bread back from their table. A couple this devout would be fasting before partaking of the Eucharist. "For the first time in our history. Our new priest hails from Bilbao." He excuses himself and returns to the tavern.

The church bell tolls eleven and I decide to attend Mass. Here, as in Ireland, church is the one place where women and men can mingle without raising eyebrows.

This church must have been beautiful once, but the soot of centuries has obscured its elegance. Typical of the Renaissance style, Doric columns hold up the high ceiling. The candlelight from the chandeliers casts a soft glow on the oaken pews and granite floors, engraved with designs and letters. I presume they memorialize important personages buried here. The stone blocks extend down the aisle from the altar almost all the way to the vestibule, near the back pew where I sit. Niches on the walls hold sculpted figures, yet the most impressive sculpture stands between two marble columns at the altar: Our Lady of Sorrows. It looks practically new. The tears on her cheek, the clasped hands on her bosom, and her blue headdress lined with gold—they shimmer by the light of the tall candles perched on gold-plated candlesticks on either side of the altar.

Perhaps because it is in Castilian, Mass is poorly attended. The couple from Barcelona sit beside a man who appears to be in his sixties, accompanied by a little girl. Middle-aged men in blue pants and white cotton shirts, typical of the peasant class, sit scattered in the pews, sitting beside women (presumably, their wives). Elderly women occupy the front row on the right side, harkening me back to the Masses I attended as a child in Ireland. Two pews before me sits Doña Carmen, Old Simon's wife. A sturdy matron draped in a black dress and a waist-length mantilla cascading from a comb atop her hair, she holds a lapis lazuli rosary in her gloved hands.

The homily reminds me of why I stopped going to Mass. Instead of elaborating on God's love and compassion featured in both readings and the Gospel, Father Itcea delivers a hagiography of Bernadette of Soubirous. Now he launches into a discussion of a recent exhumation of her remains.

"I have it on good authority," he says, "that the Vatican has ratified a report on the state of Bernadette's body. This will corroborate previous medical reports that her body has remained intact since her death forty-eight years ago. This latest report was written by a Doctor Comte, published in an important medical journal, *Bulletin de l'Association Médicale de Notre-Dame de Lourdes*."

He doesn't translate the French title. The priest pauses dramatically before quoting from the text in an officious tone.

I would have liked to open the left side of the thorax to take the ribs as relics and then remove the heart, which I am certain must have survived. It would have been rather difficult to try to get at the heart without doing noticeable damage.

Oh, no! He's going to describe the exhumation. I can stomach it, though, having witnessed many atrocities during the Great War.

The Mother Superior had expressed a desire for the saint's heart to be kept together with the whole body. I contented myself with removing the two right ribs which were more accessible.

"*Su corazón?* Her heart?" The little girl cries out before she's shushed. My own heart goes out to her, that she should be subjected to such violent imagery. And in Mass, where she should be finding succor.

Father Itcea ignores the outcry and intones:

What struck me during this examination, of course, was the state of perfect preservation of the skeleton, the fibrous tissues of the muscles (still supple and firm), of the ligaments, and of the skin, and above all the totally unexpected state of the liver after almost fifty years. One would have thought this organ would have decomposed or hardened to a chalky consistency. Yet it was soft and almost normal in consistency.

The old man beside the little girl puts his arm around her and whispers something to her.

"The incorruptible state of Bernadette's body so many years after her death proves the Virgin Mary did in fact appear to Bernadette, no matter what the cynics claim," Father Itcea says. "And it also proves that we must heed her words, and her purpose when she appears: to inspire us to defend our religion!"

I have had enough but know I cannot leave Mass early without offending Father Itcea. I let his words blur and glance at the other parishioners. From my place in the last pew, I cannot see their faces, but most sit as still as statues, like victims of Medusa's stare turned to stone.

Except for Doña Carmen. She rocks to and fro slowly, her rosary dangling from her raised hands.

"We must do as Our Lady bids us." She points to the statue altar. "Or she will come again, holding a sword dripping in blood!"

"Ez, Ez, Ez!" Blanca shouts. "No, no! Don't cut it out! Don't cut it out!" Crossing her arms tightly against her chest, she thrashes against the ropes that tie her down on the bed. The sheets are wet with her sweat and tears.

"Please!" she pleads. "Don't take out my heart!"

She peers into the darkness, pierced only by the white apron the doctor wears and the candle on the nightstand. He laughs as he sharpens his knife against a stone, the same knife Aita uses for pig killing every winter. Blanca screams, making as high-pitched a sound as the pigs' squealing when the blood bursts from their throats.

"Have mercy! Ama Maite Maria, save me!" She struggles to bring her knees against the approaching blade, but the ties hold them back. "I promise to do whatever you ask!"

"It's too late for that!" the doctor says. "Not even Christ himself can save you now!"

Blanca shuts her eyes and braces for the first cut.

Instead, a gentle hand touched her cheek.

"Shh . . . shh." She recognized her brother's voice. "You had a bad dream." Cruz wiped her damp forehead and placed a kiss there. "You're safe now." He tucked Rosa close to her chest. Xuriko bolted in and took her place at Blanca's feet. "Everything is all right."

Blanca wept in relief, yet the images from her bad dream still haunted her. *Ama Maite Maria*, she prayed silently, *please give me the courage to do your will.*

CHAPTER SIX

January 23, 1931
NOBILITY CELEBRATES KING ALFONSO'S
NAME DAY—by G.U.

F ather Itcea grinned at the headlines of the *Diario de Navarra*. While censorship still reigned throughout Spain, the Crown would have no reason to keep this news from the people. He settled into the soft leather of his chair.

Nobility and monarchists celebrated today King Alfonso's Name Day, the Feast of San Ildefonsus, with a colorful display of loyalty to the monarchy. In a five-hour ceremony beginning at noon, King Alfonso, seated on his throne in the Crown Room, received many admirals, generals, cardinals and grandees. Outside, crowds of spectators watched the flower of Old Spain arrive, many in magnificent horse carriages. Silver and gold helmets and colored plumes flashed in the sun, and uniforms of every possible combination of colors were seen.

The reminder of this saint and the pageantry lifted Father Itcea's spirits. He felt a special affinity with Ildefonsus. Like himself, the saint had come from a prominent family and had had a zealous devotion to the Virgin Mary. One December morning in 665, Ildefonsus—by then, the bishop of the Cathedral of Toledo—led his congregation in singing hymns to the Virgin Mary during Mass. Suddenly, light flooded the church and his parishioners fled in fear. Ildefonsus stayed inside and kept singing, until the Virgin Mary descended from heaven and took a seat on the altar throne before him. She praised Ildefonsus for his bravery and devotion and gave him a special garment to be worn only during Marian festivities. Because of this vision, the Vatican elevated the Cathedral of Toledo to the Metropolitan See, making it the highest ecclesiastical authority in Iberia.

Father Itcea could only dream of such an apparition. He closed his eyes and recited a Latin prayer to the Virgin Mary, entreating her to appear to one of his parishioners in Indartze. Doña Carmen clearly shared his hope and undoubtedly would be honored to be the recipient of such a visitation. Yet she would know as well as he that the Virgin Mary usually appeared to young children, whose innocence and purity made them ideal empty vessels for her messages.

He flipped through the papers Gabriel from Café Ttipia had sent him and looked for news related to Bernadette of Soubirous. Perhaps more miracles had been attributed to her, or perhaps another medical report had uncovered new revelations about the integrity of her remains. Whatever the case, Father Itcea felt certain he'd find fodder for his next homily.

A headline of a different kind, in *Le Matin*, confronted him instead.

January 31, 1931
GIRLS LEAD PROTEST IN SPAIN—by G.U.

Near the heart of downtown Madrid, having whipped itself into a high pitch of excitement by shouts of "Death to the king! Hurrah for a republic!" a group 3,000 strong, led by a band of young Amazons, set off for the royal palace to protest yesterday's shooting.

The police charged the rioters and beat them with the flats of their swords. Shots were fired into the air, and the terrified rioters dived into nearby doorways.

"*Ave Maria*, pray for us!" Father Itcea grasped his Miraculous Medallion. That women led this protests shocked him. Clearly they did not deserve the beating they received. But there would always be consequences for women who didn't know their place.

Blanca giggled in excitement to find the plaza filled with so many gaily dressed people. They chatted and laughed as they hurried to the booths selling everything from cheese, roasted chestnuts, and churros and hot chocolate to bolts of cloth, engraved walking sticks, and wooden toys. Not even the smell of manure from the fattened pigs for sale bothered her. Music from flutes, tambourines, guitars, and button-accordions mingled with the ringing of church bells. Older girls huddled in groups, flirting with boys who crossed their paths. Boys and young men in white pants and shirts took turns hitting a handball against the *pilota* court, practicing for the games later that afternoon. Older men and women sat on wooden benches near the handball court or drank their beverages at small tables in the shade.

"*Guazen!* Let's go!" Blanca said to Cruz, wanting to see the toys and trinkets up close, even if they couldn't afford to buy anything. Then she felt Aita's hand on hers. She put her arm around her father's waist and slowed her pace.

"Here, Aita." She moved toward the chairs under a tree. "This will be a good spot to watch the dancing. Maybe Cruz can find Ama."

"Good idea." Cruz winked at her. "I think I know where she might be." He made his way across the plaza to Malkorra.

"*Esker mila,*" Blanca's father said to her. "Thank you. I'll miss doing the *mutil-dantza* myself. I know your brother felt nervous about standing in for our family in the boys' dance."

"He'll have to practice hard to be as good as you!" Blanca hoped she sounded brighter than she felt. Only last year Aita had led this important dance that opened the village festival. She recalled the pride on her father's face as he answered the musicians' call to form the single-file line. The oldest male dancer in this valley, he'd led the line in a series of dances counterclockwise around the plaza. Blanca had felt so happy joining in at the clap-clap-clap that signaled the circling dancers to change the direction of their movements as they snapped their fingers, their arms raised in the air.

"It's starting!" Blanca nudged Aita. The *txistulari*, the player of the Basque flute, played a few notes. Beside him, another man kept rhythm on a drum held up by a strap around his neck. One by one, men wearing black berets, blue cotton pants, and long-sleeved white shirts with collars filed into a line. The oldest among them had about sixty years, five years younger than Aita. He tipped his beret to Blanca's father before taking his place at the head of the line, followed by dancers ever younger in age. Blanca waved to the littlest one. He seemed to have only five years.

First came Blanca's favorite part of the dance. The dancers used white kerchiefs to "hold hands" to make "bridges." The first man in the line, the *aurresku,* and the man right behind him held up their arms linked with their kerchiefs, and all the other men had to hurry under this bridge before the dance could begin.

"It's a fine group," Blanca's father said, "and Toribio will do a good job as *aurresku.*"

"He learned from the best, Aita." Blanca squeezed his hand. "You'll see. You'll be back next year."

"*Jaunak nahirik,*" her father said. "If God wills it."

Blanca looked around at the men and boys doing the dance, following each other as they went under the bridge. She counted them silently as they emerged on the other side: two, four, six, eight, ten, twelve . . . though when the thirteenth dancer tried to cross under the bridge, Toribio and the dancer behind him brought their arms down so that he could not pass. The boy looked to be a few years older than Blanca.

"*Agota zikina!* You dirty *agota!*" The *aurresku* cried out, and gasps rose from the crowd. The *txistulari* stopped playing his flute. The drummer banged on his drum and walked off the plaza, followed by the line of dancers.

"*Kanporat!*" Toribio yelled. "Out he goes!"

"What's happening?" Blanca asked her father. "Why won't they let that boy do the dance?"

"They say he's an *agota*—a dirty leper."

"He doesn't look like a leper!" From Mass, Blanca knew splotches covered the skin of lepers and lumps swelled their faces. This boy didn't look like that. Chestnut brown hair spilled out from under his black beret. Humiliation reddened his pale cheeks, and tears moistened his eyes.

Children in the crowd took up Toribio's command: "*Kan-po-rat! Kan-po-rat!*"

Some clapped in rhythm to the chant: "Out he goes! Out he goes!"

The boy's shoulders shook on his solid frame, and Blanca could now see the wrinkles on his shirt and pants, as if he had no mother or sister to iron them.

Gaixoa! she thought. *The poor thing!* She started to walk toward him. A tug at her skirt held her back.

"*Aski!*" Aita shouted at the men in a voice Blanca barely recognized. "That's enough!" He let go of Blanca's skirt and leaned on his cane to rise, and the chant died down. This only made the drum sound louder as the line of dancers made its way to the outskirts. Its pounding echoed against the walls of the church and every house around the plaza.

Blanca kneeled beside her father. "Thank you for making them stop," she whispered. "Do you know that boy?"

"His name is Refugio." He sighed. "I knew his father-that-was, as well. So long as I danced as *aurresku*, I could keep the bridge from falling over him and his boy. I thought I could count on Toribio to do the same and keep everyone else from finding out they're *agotas*."

"Is something wrong with them?" Blanca remembered the *agotas* from the song Aita had sung, but it didn't say why people didn't like them.

"Some say they descend from the lepers we hear about in the Bible. That their sickness is punishment for worshipping the devil."

This boy didn't look like a leper to Blanca; though if he worshipped the devil, she wouldn't be able to tell by looking at him. Maybe this was what the

Blessed Mother meant when she told her to *gaizkatu* Spain. Maybe Blanca was supposed to help her rid Spain of bad people—*gaiztoak*—like unbelievers.

"Do you think *agotas* worship the devil?" Blanca asked.

"It doesn't matter what I think, my girl," Aita said, his voice low. "Remember what I told you when you thought you saw that vision on Aranzibia Hill? It can be dangerous if you see or say things other people don't like. Whatever you believe, keep it to yourself, act like everybody else."

I cannot believe what I just witnessed, and yet I can.

What cruelty! To demean the boy like that! I take up my fiddle case and put my instrument inside it. I'd looked forward to playing along with the musicians here today to celebrate Maria Gurrutxetegia's day. The Vatican hasn't declared her a saint, yet the people of this valley consider her a martyr and that's enough reason to celebrate. So many people coming from out of town gives me the perfect opportunity to gather more songs and elicit more opinions for my impending deadline. But this incident has spoiled my mood. I decide to return to my lodgings.

I shake my head that people still discriminate against the *agotas* so openly. Caireann had told me about them. Like the "travelers" in Ireland, *agotas* are scapegoated for any number of social ills. Blamed for spreading diseases like leprosy among people and foot-and-mouth diseases among horses, they have had to live in isolated neighborhoods and socialize primarily with each other. Not even allowed to attend Mass with the other villagers, they have had to enter the church through separate *agota* doors. Next time I'm near Our Lady of Sorrows, I'll see if the church has such a door.

Yet the festivities go on. Merchants call out their wares from their booths, villagers visit with each other as they peruse the food and household items on offer, children run around. The smells of roasting chestnuts and pig-on-a-spit fill the air. Old Simon moves briskly between his customers on the patio outside Bar Herria.

Young men climb up the balcony on the city hall building to hang the flag of Indartze. Into the stone on the wall behind them is carved a coat of arms representing a soldier in battle. A medieval helmet sits atop a battle shield filled with squares, like a chessboard. I notice now that family crests festoon many a facade and lintel around the plaza, to beautiful effect. Likely all made by *agotas*. They are permitted to work only with stone, wood, and metal—materials that cannot transmit disease.

"If they only knew," I mutter.

Reedy notes from an accordion interrupt my thoughts. The accordion player belts out a song, and men and children across the square join along. I recognize it as the song Old Simon translated for me about Maria Gurrutxetegia. Considerably more upbeat than the version Old Simon sang for me, the tempo lightens my mood. There must be hundreds of people here. Most of them had nothing to do with the expulsion of the *agota* boy.

I light a fresh cigarette and walk quickly toward the musicians, fiddle case under my arm. I think I'll play along after all.

The singers for the *inhauterriak*, the carnival right before Lent, would be coming soon, and Blanca looked forward to their visit. She especially needed the festivities this year after watching her father's health worsen, those mean people kicking out the *agota* boy from the dance, and the disturbing dream about her heart being cut out.

Blanca listened for the knock at the door as she shelled walnuts in the attic. Then she heard the voices approach.

Jende onak, huna gu huna gu	Good people, we come
Kantatu nahi dinagu	To sing this song
Usaia begiratu eta aditu	To witness and learn
Santa Agataren kondu	About Santa Agata

They were here! She ran down the stairs, grabbed her coat and kerchief from the peg on the wall, and threw them on before opening the door.

A group of children stood at the threshold, bundled up in woolen coats. The girls wore scarves over their hair and the boys wore black caps. Each of them held a walking stick, which they struck on the ground as they sang.

Kintiano pretora gaixtoa	Evil Emperor Kintaino
Hartaz agradatua	Found her agreeable
Gan zitzaion neskaren etxera	He went to the girl's house
Ohaidetzat biltzera	To take her to his bed

The words didn't fit with the mood of the tune, though Blanca was enjoying its rhythm. An older boy and girl took a step forward, singing a line in turn as the others pounded their canes.

Agata, Kristau ona haiz ala?	Agata, are you a Christian?
Ba eta nahi ere	Yes, and that is my wish
Ez zain desohore	Aren't you ashamed?
Ohore baizik nere	No, it's an honor

Then the children sang together again, pounding their sticks even harder.

Jo dute ukabilka	They struck her repeatedly
Odola burrustaka	Made her drip blood, head to toe
Agata iduri du arroka	Agata was like a rock
Deusek ezin kordoka	Nothing could dissuade her

Ostiko, laido zikin-zikinan	They kicked her on the dirty straw
Azote, ur irakin	Whipped her with red-hot ferns
Larrutze su-puntekin	Skinned her with hot pokers
Nork iraun hoiek denekin?	Who could survive all that?

Blanca drew back at the horror of these words. Yet the older boy and girl sang their parts, smiling.

Ukan hor berehala	Immediately renounce
Jesus hire idola!	Jesus as your idol!
Ez dirot sekulan abandona	I will never abandon
Ene gatik hil dena!	He who died for me!

The other children stepped forward, and all sang in one voice.

Besoak lotuak, bihurturik	Arms tied up
Zangoak leherturik	Her legs shattered
Bularrak urraturik, Agata	Her breasts cut off
Hor datza hil-utzirik	Agatha was left to die

Estatu hortan bada, gaixoa	In that state, poor thing
Uzten dute etxera	They took her home
Gan dezaten hiltzera	To die
Bere jenden artera	Among her people

This song told the most terrible story Blanca had ever heard: Agata was still alive when they cut her up, then they left her for dead!

The children looked at her expectantly. Blanca knew she was supposed to give them treats to thank them for this Ash Wednesday reminder of a martyr's imitation of Christ's sacrifice.

But she slammed the door without giving them anything.

Settled into his leather chair, Father Itcea eagerly read through the newspaper clippings sent by Gabriel. They'd piled up over several days as the priest prepared his homily for Sunday. He'd decided to focus on the doctrine of the Immaculate Conception, the idea that the Virgin Mary was conceived without sin. The girls and women of Indartze should aspire to be like her, not those radical women leading protests across Spain.

The headline of the first article made his blood boil.

February 8, 1931
SPAIN READY TO TURN REPUBLICAN
Self-Government Possible without Red Menace—By G.U.

"Spain is ready for a democratically elected government and self-rule," I was told today by a government official who spoke on condition of anonymity. "The disorders of the last few weeks," he explained, "were but a safety valve effusion caused by the enormous pressure of discontent. Public confidence can be restored only by summoning a constituent assembly to frame a new constitution."

Father Itcea grasped his Miraculous Medallion. He had heard rumors of what such a constitution would include from his "modern" friends in Bilbao. It would nationalize Catholic landholdings and tax others. Fanatics even called for the dissolution of Catholic religious orders. Such a constitution would destroy the moral and political foundations of this country.

"I have not the slightest fear that if a republic were instituted, it would suffer the fate of Russia," said the official. "People who say that have no knowledge of Spain. Her economic and social problems, totally different from Russia's, would make a Soviet regime impossible. We have neither class hatred nor preparation and authoritative direction. Nor, above all, do we have the discipline among the masses required for such a government."

That's certainly true. While disciplined when it came to their livelihoods, Basques did not exhibit the self-sacrifice required for political transformation.

"On the other hand," he said, "the Great War so upset the traditions of Europe and the entire world that the people of Spain view a republic as offering hope for the fulfillment of their ideas. The old idea of the king above all has given way to a feeling that the country is above the king, and if the king cannot rule in the interests of the country, he must abdicate."

He continued, "Republican ideas have penetrated the masses. Both workers and farmers look favorably on republicanism, and even the army would be willing to accept a republic. In view of these facts, I am confident that Spain is ready to accept a liberal, democratic, parliamentary republic, for which able leaders would easily be found. It is the only solution possible if Spain is to continue to live in peace and order."

"Only God brings us peace and order!" Father Itcea would have to move quickly to protect his parishioners from these ideas. Martial law would not keep this news from his parishioners forever. Indartze lay only five miles from France, and parishioners and villagers crossed the border frequently to visit relatives or buy goods, exchanging gossip and ideas.

In fact, advertisements in the local paper *Gure Txoko—Our Corner*—often motivated such visits. Father Itcea looked through the back pages of the morning edition. Advertisements for myriad products (many from France) covered the pages: Madame X slimming aides for women and the Fortificante Express body-building regimes for men; Americanas Fantasía trousers; the Etcheberria bookshop and music store; the FLIP pulverizer that promised to kill bugs faster; a hair salon that guaranteed women the perfect "romantic wave" for only ten pesetas. Obituaries mixed among a solicitation for a Basque-speaking pharmacy assistant, statistics on agricultural production, marketing by dentists and optometrists. And just what Father Itcea hoped for: short articles such as "A Word from the Basques of Madrid," "Basque Nationalism," and "Women's Lives."

Beside the last of these was a photograph of a young woman in a sleeveless white dress, a black sash cutting across from her right shoulder to her left hip. No medallion honoring the Virgin Mary or Jesus dangled from her bare neck; her only jewelry was a string of pearls wound around her wrist. No mantilla covered her short hair, which was pulled back, revealing eyebrows and lids darkened with liner and thin lips covered in lipstick. The photo was captioned "Señorita República."

"Not here!" Father Itcea took up his pen in alarm. He hoped it was not too late to battle against this promotion of the "modern" woman, a woman who would surely undermine the family traditions that held Basque society together. He would write in favor of traditional Basque customs, so inextricably tied to the Church. *Gure Txoko* was read widely in Indartze, even by people who never set foot in Our Lady of Sorrows; he'd passed many men reading it in the plaza when they should have been on their way to Mass. He would use a pseudonym or catchy byline the way many other writers did.

The church bells tolled. He stretched and looked out into the plaza. And it came to him. He would write under the caption *Jaingoikoa eta Lege Zaharra*— God and the Old Laws. Emblazoned on buildings, coats of arm, and flags, this had been the motto of the Basques for centuries. But these days it was conspicuously missing from the public domain, and it was time someone brought it back.

Blanca stared at the ceiling from her bed, waiting for the shape of the beams to emerge in the shuttered room. She usually fell asleep easily for her afternoon nap. She heard the clock chime three, then realized she didn't hear Aita snoring. It usually lulled her to sleep. She threw off her bedclothes, smoothed her blouse and skirt, and slowly opened her bedroom door. She looked down the hall to her parents' bedroom; the door was ajar.

I wonder if he snuck out again? She tiptoed down the wooden stairs, hoping to keep them from squeaking. At the foot of the stairs she put on her *abarkak*, her leather work shoes, and then closed the front door gently behind her. She hurried the few feet to her father's workshop, really just a woodshed attached to the barn that sheltered the cows and sheep.

Blanca looked forward to the conversation she would have with Aita there. He always had such interesting stories to share about his time as a lumberjack on the French side of the Basque Country or how he'd met Ama through his business dealings with her father. He wouldn't let Blanca use any of the big tools—the saw or the axe—yet she liked to hand him the hammer, screwdrivers, or nails he used for the chairs and tables he made. Sometimes he would make toys for her, like the wooden doll he'd made for her last birthday.

Her hand on the door latch, Blanca took one last look to tidy herself and noticed that mud caked her shoes. She sat down, looking for a stick or some hay to pick the mud off. An unfamiliar boy's voice talking to her father directed her attention inside the woodshed.

Who could that be? Aita never had visitors.

Blanca lay on her belly so that she could peek through the gap under the door. The *agota* boy! He had his back to Blanca, though she would know that curly hair anywhere. He had no cap and wore a shirt and pants that were too big for him, but clean. Cruz's old clothes!

"*Ederra duk!* Beautiful!" Aita picked up what seemed to be a large slab of wood and stood it up on the table. "A couple more days' work and it should be ready to sell."

More days? How long had the boy been working with her father?

"*Esker mile*—thank you," the *agota* boy said. "I couldn't have done it without your help."

"Bah!" Aita said. "You're a natural! Just like your father-that-was."

The boy took time to answer, and his voice was barely audible when he did. "I hope one day I can be as good a carpenter as he was," he said.

Blanca's father stepped closer to the boy and his voice dropped as well. "I have no doubt, Refugio. Your father, Antonio, was a man of few words, but he had only praise for you. With more practice, you'll be the best carpenter in the whole valley."

Bleating from the barn roused Blanca to her feet. She'd have to lead the sheep to pasture soon. And clearly, Aita preferred to spend time with this new boy rather than with her.

Setting my fiddle case on my lap, I take a seat outside Father Itcea's office. Too low for a man of my height, the chair aligns my gaze directly with a simple wooden crucifix. The wooden Christ has the stocky build of a peasant made strong by a lifetime of labor in the fields. His head tips forward as if weighed down by his crown of thorns. His brown eyes look upon me with a warmth that feels more real than anything I have experienced from actual clergy, or even from anyone with strong religious convictions.

Still, priests often provide the best examples of songs and local knowledge that my readers appreciate, and I've not yet had a chance to engage Father Itcea in conversation. I'd hoped that our paths would cross naturally as we went about our business. Apparently he doesn't frequent Bar Herria or spend time mingling in the town square. I've attended Mass only the one time. Last weekend's fete in honor of Maria Gurrutxetegia has finally provided me with a good excuse to seek him out.

The clock pings quarter past two, and the priest emerges from his office. His jaw tightens when he sees me, and I wonder if I erred in showing up without an appointment. Then he extends his hand. "*Buenos días*, William."

I return the greeting and follow him into his office. Dominating the room is a massive wooden desk piled with large envelopes, articles, and books. A simple crucifix hangs over the window facing the plaza. On the wall opposite hangs a framed photograph of pilgrims at the grotto at Lourdes.

"How nice to see you again." Father Itcea sits upright in his high-backed leather chair and adjusts his round-rimmed spectacles. I sit in the simple wicker-and-wood chair for visitors. "I wasn't sure you were still here. I haven't seen you around."

Or at Mass on Sundays, perhaps he means.

"Oh, I've been out and about," I say. "I've enjoyed my time in Indartze. Though as a musician, I find weekends best for visiting other small towns and hearing their songs."

While not strictly true, it's not a complete falsehood. I have been back and forth to several towns since I've been here, albeit for other purposes. Residual Catholic guilt prevents me from lying outright to a priest.

"Ah," he says. "To what do I owe the pleasure of your visit?"

I open my case and take out the notes I've tucked away under my fiddle. "I hope you might provide more background to a song I've collected here, about Maria Gurrutxetegia? Old Simon translated the words for me, yet there must be more to her story if people still sing about her after four hundred years."

The priest's brow furrows.

"I confess I don't know much about this Maria," he says after a long pause. "I arrived here only a short time ago, and I am still getting to know my current parishioners."

"Of course, addressing the spiritual needs of the living is most important." I ramble on, as I do during awkward moments. "And I'm sure the claims about her curing people were just fueled by alcohol . . ."

"What's that now?" He touches my arm. "Tell me everything you have heard."

After William's visit, Father Itcea realized he should be investigating the local girl Maria for sainthood, not Bernadette Soubirous of Lourdes. Any priest who spoke French could advocate for Bernadette. Only a Basque speaker like him could make the case for Maria.

Her devotees abounded. Today the priest looked forward to fleshing out his notes about the miracles they'd attributed to Maria. For context, he'd already made a list of the historical facts of her case:

1. Maria was only fifteen when burned at the stake as a witch, denying the accusations to the end.

2. Through the agony of the flames, she prayed Psalm 37, the Old Testament's answer to the problem of evil. Her last words supposedly were "Do good and dwell forever."

3. A ballad had been written about Maria's martyrdom at the stake, simply titled *"Jende Onak, Huna Gu"*—"Good People, Here We Have," in the unhelpful tradition of Basque songwriters to name songs after the first line. Father Itcea had likely heard the song at the village festival, but he didn't realize its significance. (The people of Indartze broke out into song with great frequency to opine on the most mundane of matters, though now the priest knew to pay more attention.) Although the feast day was St. Agata's Day by the Roman Catholic calendar, the locals had for centuries unofficially celebrated it as Maria's saint's day.

4a. Despite the Church's prohibitions to the contrary, a young Jesuit was rumored to have saved Maria's ashes and given them to Father Zabaleta, then rector of Our Lady of Sorrows, who witnessed Maria's burning.

4b. Some believe the ashes were buried deep within the bowels of the church. The previous rector had gone mad looking for them.

The insane priest had shared his suspicions with his altar boys, some of whom shared his beliefs. (Of course, the names of these now-grown men were also kept under wraps.)

4c. A more popular theory as to the whereabouts of Maria's ashes was that they were sprinkled into a spring in the mountains, which had subsequently acquired curative powers for those who drank from or bathed in it.

The last point interested the priest most. Maria's followers claimed miracles had occurred after praying upon her remains. William could not provide more detail, as he was extremely drunk when he heard the stories.

Even though these events spanned centuries, Maria's miracles had not been brought to the Vatican's attention. Likely her obscure language and the remoteness of this town did not help matters.

Father Itcea took up his pen, determined to put this right.

CHAPTER EIGHT

Blanca waited for her brother on a bench outside Our Lady of Sorrows. Cruz had gone to settle on a price for their pigs.

"*Non hago?*" Blanca said to herself. "Where are you?" She looked toward Bar Herria, where Cruz would often go after running errands, hoping to see him coming out.

Then she heard voices yelling from inside the bar and a crowd spilling through its doors. They pushed a boy through and clawed at him, tearing his clothes.

Blanca craned her neck to see. It was the *agota* boy, Refugio.

A man yelled at Refugio, "What have you done to him?"

"You dirty *agota!*" another one screamed.

"Mur-der-er! Mur-der-er!" chanted a boy. Others joined him. "*Hil-tzai-le! Hil-tzai-le!*"

That can't be right. Refugio was just a poor orphan.

Some boys rushed toward the crowd as if to join in, and Blanca's heart pounded at what might happen next.

"*Aski!*" Cruz dropped a package as he raced across the plaza. "That's enough!" The crowd froze in place. Refugio covered his head with his hands.

Blanca picked up the package Cruz had dropped and slowly inched toward the crowd.

"What's going on here?" Cruz kneeled beside Refugio, wiping the tears and blood from the boy's face.

People in the crowd looked at each other.

Cruz spotted her. "Blanca, did you see what happened?"

"I, uh—"

The angry stare of the crowd bore down on her.

"Well, I was over there and—"

"—What does she know?" A man's voice interrupted her. "She's just a girl!"

"She was too far away!"

"She couldn't see anything!"

Cruz tried to shush the crowd, but the yelling drowned out his voice. He stayed squatting next to the *agota* boy.

"*Ixo!* Quiet!" Father Itcea's voice boomed across the plaza as he hurried toward them.

"What is going on?"

Cruz sat Refugio up, dusted himself off, and stood up. "You will have to ask these men, Father Itcea." He took his cap off. "I was coming out from the butcher's and saw this crowd beating this boy and yelling at him."

"Is that so?" The priest looked from one man to another.

"We had a good reason, Father," one of them said. "Three days ago, my brother went missing. He has eighteen years but he has the mind of a child." The man twirled his index finger in a circle by his temple.

Father Itcea nodded. "Go on."

"Well, because of his, um, childlike ways, he's never been allowed to go beyond the sheepfold on his own. Yet he went out to bring in the sheep on Monday, and we haven't seen him since."

"And you have reason to suspect this boy of having a hand in the disappearance?" Father Itcea asked.

"It's not just a disappearance, Father!" The man broke into tears. "This morning we found that dirty *agota* sleeping in the sheepfold, his clothes covered with blood. We fear it is my brother's, for we also found this on him." The man took out a switchblade. "Just like my brother's!"

"This is pigs' blood." Refugio touched his shirt. "I don't even know your brother!"

"Then why did you run?" the man asked. "Only guilty people run away."

"Father, if I may make a suggestion?" A familiar woman's voice rose above the noise, and Blanca's spirits lifted. There stood the beautiful young woman from Malkorra. The sun shone behind her straw-colored hair. Her voice lilted softly, yet all the men in the crowd craned toward it.

The priest signaled his permission.

"I am so sorry to hear this man's brother is lost. I would be worried about him too," she said. "Perhaps an attempt should be made to find him outside of Indartze before assuming the worst?"

"He is not capable of going far on his own!" the man protested.

"That may well be," said the young woman. "Shouldn't we know for certain before condemning this boy?"

The crowd fell silent, all eyes on her. Blanca glanced at Cruz. He looked at the woman too, his cheeks flushed.

"Caution is the wiser path here," Father Itcea said. "You"—he pointed to Cruz. "Work with this man to organize a search party for his brother. Refugio, you come with me. The civil authorities will keep you until these men have concluded their search."

Blanca had heard terrible things about what the police would do to people in their custody, whether guilty or not. Refugio seemed relieved. It occurred to her that he likely had been sleeping in the man's sheepfold because he had nowhere else to go.

She took one more look at Refugio. The poor thing. He had not done anything to the missing man, Blanca could feel it. If only she could find a way to prove it.

Guilt still gnaws at me days later. Clearly eager to make his mark in the Church by "finding" a saint, Father Itcea expressed gratitude for the details I provided him about Maria Gurrutxetegia's martyrdom (execution, more accurately). We finally established the rapport I've been hoping for. When we parted, he took my hand in both of his and said he owed me a favor. And I plan on keeping him to his word.

Yet, I did not tell him all I know.

I go to my closet and retrieve a cardboard box I've secreted there behind my fiddle case and knapsack. Replacing the Gaulois at my lips, I set the box on my bed. In the box is everything left behind at Bar Herria by the priest who'd lost his mind. Old Simon had safeguarded it for him as promised. The poor priest had been taken away to an asylum before his treasures could be returned to him.

"My wife doesn't even know this exists," Old Simon had said. "I worry what she'd do if she found it, now that she's so involved with the Unión Patriótica." This group hopes to insert conservative Catholic beliefs into the government.

The box contains photographs, correspondence with international postmarks, prayers and petitions from parishioners going back fifty years, religious medallions, and small crosses made of hemp or straw. Most interesting of all is a faded blueprint of Our Lady of Sorrows. And a list of altar boys who'd assisted the priest in his quest to find Maria's ashes. Among their names is that of Cruz, the young man who helped me get my bearings when I first arrived in this town. I haven't seen him around lately. Looks like we have some catching up to do.

It had been two weeks since Refugio had been taken to the barracks, and with each passing day Blanca feared for his safety. Cruz and his search party hadn't found the man who had disappeared, and she began to doubt her certainty about Refugio's innocence.

It was Palm Sunday. Seated in church, Blanca knew she should be paying attention to the homily, about the Last Supper and how Jesus sacrificed himself for our sins. She sat with her father at her left as always, though Cruz's usual place at her right was taken by her mother. Her brother had stayed out late looking for the missing man, he said, and had stayed home to catch up on his sleep.

"It's the responsorial psalm." Blanca's mother nudged her. "My God, my God—"

"—why."

"Why have you abandoned me?" Blanca finished the supplication with her mother and sat up, determined not to miss another word. Without Cruz to come early to save their usual pew, she and her parents had ended up in the first row, where only the elderly ladies sat by choice. Blanca had never sat so close to Our Lady of Sorrows, and no one blocked her view of the altar. She felt as if she saw the statue for the first time. The glass tears on the Blessed Mother's reddened cheeks shone in the candlelight.

"She looks so real," Blanca whispered. She gazed at the statue as the words of the psalm floated up:

"My God, my God, why have you abandoned me?"

She thought about Refugio, all by himself in that cell. No father or mother to look out for him.

"My God, my God, why have you abandoned me?"

Blanca's heart beat in time to the response. There must be something she could do. The knot in her stomach tightened. Somehow she knew the missing man was safe. If she could find him, she could also free Refugio.

A latecomer entered through the side door and a breeze snuck in with him. A shiver tingled the back of Blanca's neck and pulsed up to the crown of her head. She heard a soft voice say, "Refugio." It sounded as if it came from Our Lady of Sorrows. Blanca looked more closely at the statue's face. The lips seemed to part and repeat, "Refugio."

Blanca looked at her father and mother, then at the other parishioners nearby. None of them seemed to have heard the voice. They had their eyes closed and rapped their fists on their chests as they repeated the responsorial psalm.

Am I imagining things?

"Refugio," the statue said a third time. Blanca faced the holy image and nodded. She thought more deeply about what this word *Refugio* meant: "Refuge."

Where do you find refuge when you feel afraid? Our Lady of Sorrows seemed to ask her.

Blanca used to go into the caves on the outskirts of Indartze whenever she needed comforting. She found it soothing inside. Nice and quiet, the thick rock walls kept the caves cool in summer, warm in winter. A brook inside provided cool water to drink, and its babbling sound calmed her. In places where the sun poked through, green patches brightened the limestone. And many birds fluttered in and out, practicing their songs.

Blanca used to go into the caves until she heard the scary stories about what happened with the witches there. If the missing man was indeed "simple," perhaps his family and friends had kept those stories from him. Perhaps he had entered the caves.

The congregation finished the psalm and fell quiet again. Our Lady of Sorrows smiled at Blanca. The knot in Blanca's stomach went away. She knew for certain now the missing man hid somewhere in the caves. She couldn't wait to tell Cruz.

No one else would listen to a little girl talking to a statue.

Easter Sunday approached and Father Itcea paced his office, preparing his homily. He wanted his parishioners to more fully appreciate the significance of Christ's resurrection, particularly during these politically troubling times. Soon Spain would hold municipal elections, and without his guidance, Father Itcea knew, the men of his congregation would have no understanding of the stakes: the sovereignty of the Word of God itself. If the Communists and Anarchists had their way, Spain would become a republic where the Catholic Church and the state would be separated. The institution of marriage would fall under the purview of the state, which meant that divorce could also become legal.

The priest would not stand for this; he shuddered at the laws men would pass if left to their own devices. The laity had no understanding that the Church had brought about the most perfect society that had ever existed on this earth. Father Itcea took it as a sign from heaven that the second reading for this year's Easter Mass spoke directly to this point. He intoned, "A reading from the First Letter of Paul to the Colossians," then continued:

Brothers and Sisters:

If then you were raised with Christ, seek what is above, where Christ is seated at the right hand of God. Think of what is above, not of what is on earth.

Father Itcea would love to proffer a sophisticated exegesis of the last line in particular, but he would have to simplify the message to a level understandable to his humble congregants. He looked out the window to see two young men playing *pilota* while another waited on the sidelines. He recognized the spectator as Cruz.

The priest rapped on the window and signaled the young man to meet him in the rectory.

"Thank you for joining me." Father Itcea offered the young man a seat. "I wonder if you might help me with something."

Cruz fidgeted, his gaze darting between the office's open door and the priest's desk. "I will try, Father," he said.

"As you know, Easter is in two days, and it is my responsibility to ensure that the people of Indartze observe this holiest of holy days with the respect it deserves."

Cruz blushed, then looked at the floor. "I am sorry, Father. Is it forbidden to play *pilota* on Good Friday?"

"No, no, it is fine." Father Itcea grinned at the simplicity of the question, then realized that he did not know if the Church took a stand on this issue. He jotted down a note to ask his spiritual director on his next consultation. "I am hoping you will listen to the homily I am preparing for Easter Mass and let me know what you think."

Or if you even understand it.

Cruz sat up as parishioners were wont to do in their pews during the homily. "I will try my best," he said.

"As usual, the Gospel itself will be about how Mary Magdalene went to the tomb where Jesus's body had been taken after his crucifixion and finds the tomb empty. Normally I use this reading to emphasize how a mere woman could not recognize the Lord after he had risen from the dead. And why women are not fit to spread the Good News."

Cruz raised his eyebrows.

"This year I will be drawing primarily on the second reading." Father Itcea read Paul's Letter to the Colossians to Cruz, emphasizing the last line: "Think of what is above, not of what is on earth."

The young man nodded, though Father Itcea doubted he knew the significance of the line. He began to explain it, then thought it best to simply read the homily on its own to see if Cruz could understand it without prelude, as the parishioners would be asked to do on Sunday.

"On April twelfth," the priest read, "we men will be entrusted with the highest responsibility given to us by God. The opportunity to reaffirm our devotion to *Una España Unida por Dios*—One Spain United for God. He paused to let the words sink in, per the notation he had made to himself.

"It is our duty as men to affirm our faith in our king, Alfonso XIII, and vote for the monarchist candidates in next Sunday's election. Our king is an ideal ruler for this country. Born to the purple, he does honor to the ancient splendor of the crown he wears. He knows the science of statesmanship, proof of which is that he kept Spain out of the Great War. As he protected us from destruction, we must now protect him."

Looking up from his paper, Father Itcea noticed Cruz's eyes had glazed over. At most, Cruz was twenty years old, three years short of the minimum voting age. *The horrors of the Great War would mean nothing to that generation*, the priest thought. *He would have to appeal to them a different way.*

"King Alfonso XIII is brave and fearless. He moves freely among his people despite many assassination attempts against him. Even on his wedding day, an anarchist threw a bomb at him, hidden in a bouquet of flowers!"

His eyes round, Cruz rested his elbows on his knees.

"It is his unwavering faith in God that gives our great king the courage to face these attacks. It is this faith that his enemies—these Republicans—would wrest from the bosom of Spain. Therefore, I implore you—I command you—to vote for candidates who have pledged their loyalty to our brave King Alfonso XIII and the Catholic Spain for which he stands."

Cruz tightened his left hand into a fist, loosening the bandage there used to protect against the rock-hard *pilota*.

"I have prepared a list of acceptable monarchist candidates." Father Itcea glanced at Cruz as he looked among the papers piled on his desk. In Cruz's eyes shone the unflinching, burning attention of a political consciousness newly born.

Too bad he's not yet of age to vote, Father Itcea thought. *Spain could use young recruits like him.*

CHAPTER NINE

Blanca trudged up to Aranzibia Hill, wiping the sweat off her face with her handkerchief. *Denbora xapa*, the sticky, humid weather she hated. The air felt too close and her breaths came in short puffs. Ordinarily Blanca would be chasing frogs in the river as an excuse to jump in and keep cool.

"Blessed Mother, please appear to me," Blanca prayed. She tightened her grip on her rosary made of pearls, the one Amatxi Angeline had given her for her First Holy Communion last year. She smoothed her skirt and her hair, making sure her white ribbon was still in place. She had worn it for Easter, and she wanted to look special for the Blessed Mother.

"*Hemen naiz*—I'm here." Blanca said, then realized the Blessed Mother would already know that.

Blanca waited in the quiet and stillness, her pulse pounding at her temples.

"Blanca, my child," said a familiar voice, soft and low.

Blanca opened her eyes and stood up straight, the way she did in Mass when the priest arrived. She held her rosary against her chest. The Blessed Mother looked more beautiful than ever. The sun framed her head like a halo. She wore a crown of gold, encrusted with pearls and jewels of green and red. Red also were the roses, intermixed with white lilies, that stuck up from the crown. Similar jewels shone from the edging of her cornflower blue robe made from a thick material that looked soft enough to sleep on. Her flaxen hair flowed loosely about her shoulders.

The Blessed Mother's smile reached all the way to her brown eyes, filling Blanca's whole being with joy.

"Blanca, you must build a simple chapel, here among the four oak trees."

"Yes, Ama." Blanca wanted so much to please the beautiful, kind Mother of God. Then panic seized her. "I don't know how to build a chapel!"

"Be not afraid," the Blessed Mother said. "I shall send someone to help you."

Who? Aita could do it, but he couldn't make it up Aranzibia Hill.

"The people must have hope in the difficult times to come." The jewels in the Blessed Mother's crown blurred. The folds of her robe began to fade. "The chapel will be a refuge for the Basque people, for the faithful."

"Why me?" Blanca squeaked out the question. "No one pays any attention to me!"

"For you are pure of heart," the Blessed Mother answered. "The right words will come to you and the people will listen."

"I can't do it!" Blanca felt tears on her cheeks. "I'm not worthy!"

"I know what it is like to feel unworthy." The Blessed Mother touched Blanca's cheek. "Just as God chose a young girl like me to bear His Son, I have chosen you to carry out this mission."

The weight and honor of this responsibility overwhelmed Blanca as her shoulders slumped. Surely there must be others more suited to this task?

But she had been raised to obey her parents and honor God.

"I will try my best, Ama." Blanca tried to steady herself. Sweat coated her skin, even though the cool breeze still wafted through the trees. She felt lightheaded, but there was nowhere for her to sit. "What must I do?"

Then everything went dark.

"Blanca, please wake up." A worried boy's voice came from faraway. "Your father is worried."

This jolted Blanca awake. She found herself lying on the ground. The sky had darkened above the treetops, swaying in the breeze. Beside her holding her hand sat Refugio, his hazel eyes wide with concern.

"Oh, thank God!" he said. "I thought you'd never wake up!"

Blanca sat up. "What am I doing up here?" She looked around, then remembered.

"I could ask you the same question!" Refugio stood up and held out his hand. "Do you think you can get up?"

"I think I'm all right." Blanca pretended to focus on her footing so that she could keep looking down. How embarrassing that Refugio had found her like this.

"Take it slow," Refugio admonished. Though his hand was rough with splinters, Blanca liked how it felt. "Just sit down again if you feel dizzy."

Blanca got to her feet. "What happened?"

"Your father got anxious when you didn't come home by the time I arrived for my lesson," he said. "He said you sometimes take your time after fetching water in the morning, but never that long."

Blanca felt her cheeks flush again, that she'd troubled her father.

"When you weren't at the river, I wondered where else you could be," Refugio said. "And I remembered he'd told me you two would come up here to look for mushrooms."

Smart boy, Blanca thought. *Caring.* "Thank you for finding me."

Refugio unfastened the bota bag from his belt. "Here," he said. "Drink this. Then we'll get going."

Blanca welcomed the water as it cooled her throat. Walking beside Refugio, she recalled what the Blessed Mother had told her. Something about building a chapel here. She remembered asking her how to do that, though nothing after that.

What if the Blessed Mother had told her how to make the chapel and she'd missed it? Would she still be able to carry out her mission? What would happen if she did not?

"Do you know you talk in your sleep?" Refugio gestured for the bota bag and took a drink.

Blanca felt her cheeks flame anew. "I had no idea!"

"That's not the part I'm concerned about." Refugio pursed his lips. "My father used to talk in his sleep. At times he would even go on a walk still asleep."

"Did I do that?" Blanca felt mortified. No—she woke up right where the Blessed Mother had appeared to her.

"You had your eyes closed like you were sleeping but your mouth open, as if marveling at something. You'd say a few words, make these gestures with your hands, then nod at the sky."

"I'm so embarrassed!" Blanca said. "I must have looked like I'd lost my mind!"

"Not at all—that's the odd part." Refugio lowered his voice. "It was like it was the most normal conversation in the world, though no one else was there."

"There *was* someone else there," Blanca wanted to say.

"Maybe I talk in my sleep to my doll Rosa and that's what I thought I was doing," Blanca said. "What did I say?"

"It didn't sound like anything you would talk to a doll about," Refugio answered. "You mentioned different kinds of trees and stones. Fancy words I've heard only priests say, for the things they use for Mass."

Blanca's heart raced. This sounded like a list of things she'd need for a chapel.

"I sometimes act things out with Rosa," she said. "You said I gestured with my hands?"

"Let me show you." Refugio gave her the bota bag and his hand lingered on hers. She felt so close to him. Like to a brother.

And, also, not.

"It looked like this." Refugio put one thumb on top of the other, then interlaced the other fingers. Except his index fingers, whose tips he joined together so that they formed a point.

Or a steeple!

Refugio must be the one the Blessed Mother meant! Aita had been teaching him woodworking, the Blessed Mother had sent Refugio to find her, and he'd heard her talking to the Blessed Mother about the chapel.

Now she could carry out her mission! And she would not be alone.

After dropping my envelope off at the tobacconist that doubles as a post office, I enter Old Simon's tavern. In place of the table in the corner is an overturned wine crate. Throughout the tavern, people from town and countryside, judging from their suits and dirt ed shirtsleeves, chat rapidly among themselves in Basque and Castilian. No children in this crowd. I wonder what could bring such a varied group together.

Two young men affix on the wall a poster of a young red-headed woman with short hair. She wears a sleeveless brown dress, dangling gold earrings, and a matching necklace. A red, yellow, and purple flag, the word *Libertad* emblazed on it, drapes over her left shoulder.

I look around for a perch where I can observe whatever is about to transpire. I wend my way through the crowd toward Old Simon, behind the cash register.

"*Oye!*" I say. "Hey! Something important must be happening for so many people to come."

"Who am I to say?" Old Simon shrugs. "A longtime customer asked to hold a meeting here, and so long as they buy drinks, I don't care who they are."

"Your special red wine for me, Simon?" I put a large bill on the counter, so he knows more orders will follow.

A grin on his face, Old Simon takes the bottle off the shelf on the mirrored wall behind him. I find a place to stand at the end of the bar. From this post, I can see everything and everyone.

"*Salut!*" Old Simon hands me my glass and holds his up.

"*Gártha!*" I take a swig.

"So-fi-a! So-fi-a!" The shouts and applause from the crowd drown out our toast. People cheer as a woman makes her way toward the overturned wine crate, but I can't get a good look because everyone stands up.

Then she steps onto the crate and I catch my breath. She is the most stunning woman I have seen in this village. Perhaps twenty years old, she holds herself with the confidence of a wellborn lady. Her skirt and blouse are made of the finest fabrics.

She gestures that people should sit. She straightens her back and says, *"Dignidad! Respeto!"* Her voice booms—not what I expected from a woman of such small stature. "These are the things that a republic will bring! The dignity that comes from a fair wage!" She raises her fist. "The respect that comes from taking care of your family and your neighbors!"

The crowd roars: "Dignity! Respect!"

Then Sofia says something I can't understand and more shouting ensues. I turn to Old Simon. "Did she repeat what she said in Basque?"

"Yes," he says. "The people I know here speak only Basque."

"Hmmm," I say. "Interesting."

As the chants continue, Sofia scans her audience slowly, like a queen surveying her subjects. She holds her hand up again to quiet them.

"Dignity!" She says, arm outstretched, fingers splayed. "Respect!" She turns to take in the whole crowd, hair fanning and filled with lamplight. "We will take back what the king has taken from us! He lives in luxury in his palaces and travels the world in yachts while we struggle to buy food for our families! The king must go!"

The crowd echoes: "The king must go! The king must go!"

Sofia silences the multitude with a simple signal.

"A republic will treat us all with dignity and respect!" She points to the poster behind her. "And it will grant us the liberty we have longed for! All of us—men and women!"

More cheers erupt as Sofia translates this into Basque.

"We will not be free until we can earn our livelihoods as we wish! Until we can buy what we need with our wages!" She regards the women in the crowd. "Who knows better than the women-of-the-house how hard it is to feed a family when prices go up and up each day?"

More cries rise from the throng. The older men beside me shift in their seats and say something to each other in Basque. I look at Old Simon, hoping his expression will betray his feelings about what the men have said. His expression is inscrutable.

"We must shake off the yoke of oppression King Alfonso and the ruling classes have forced upon us! To this fight we must all lend our hands!" Sofia's eyes shine like those of the woman in the poster, as if looking forward to a brighter future. "To be free of tyranny, *all* people must have the same rights! *All* must have the same responsibilities!"

She glances at the young sentries. They take some papers from their satchels and distribute them.

"This is the proposed article to the new constitution. This is what a republic would give us!" Sofia has to raise her voice as small groups huddle together over the papers, some reading the text aloud to others.

Sofia seems to realize some people here are illiterate. "This article would grant citizens of either sex over the age of twenty-three the right to vote!"

Cries rise up.

"*Por fín!* Finally!"

"*Qué vergüenza!* Disgraceful!"

"*Qué dices, mujer?* What are you saying, woman?"

Then a low, rage-filled voice booms from the tavern door: "The place of the woman is at home, not the ballot box! Get out of here with your blasphemous talk!"

The bar falls silent and I turn with everyone toward the speaker.

It's Doña Carmen. She's cast her black mantilla off her face. She clutches a Bible against her bosom.

"God has ordained that women must do whatever their fathers and husbands say!" She glares at Sofia. "You would know this if you went to church!"

Some patrons exit the bar, but most stay put. The two young men return to Sofia's side. I maneuver toward her as well.

Sofia faces Doña Carmen, determination glowing in her eyes. "I have gone to church my whole life."

"I don't believe you!" Doña Carmen says. "No woman who has heard God's words would dare speak as you do!"

"I don't need to go to church to hear God's word," Sofia retorts. "I hear God's words in the mouths of ordinary people. I see God's works in their actions, whether they believe in God or not."

More murmurings from the crowd. Some people make the sign of the cross.

"How dare you desecrate the Word of God!" Doña Carmen responds angrily. "You're just a girl! Who are you to question the One True Church?"

"I'll tell you who I am," Sofia says. "I am the daughter of Paulo Mendiburu, the owner of the largest cement factory in Bilbao. For eighteen years I lived under his roof and followed his rules. I went to Mass each morning and believed every word the priest said. I was educated by private tutors, who taught me only those things deemed necessary for a wellborn wife and mother to know."

Sarcasm sharpens her tone. "Just enough arithmetic to pay household bills, just enough literature and languages to entertain guests, and just enough about child-rearing to know how to hire a governess."

The audience listens, enraptured by Sofia's story. Doña Carmen stands with her arms crossed over her chest, her eyes blazing.

"I was betrothed to the son of my father's best friend, who owned an iron works," she says. "I did not love the man, but I was told duty was more important than love . . ."

Her voice trails off.

"After all," Sofia changes her tone, as if speaking as a man, "the Virgin Mary did not choose Joseph. She just did as God commanded."

"And she is the most blessed among women," Doña Carmen shoots back. "The model of female perfection: obedient to God, devoted to her Son, dedicated to serving others! Why should you want anything else?"

Sofia reaches out toward Doña Carmen. "Yes, God gave me these hands so that I may serve others. Did he not also give me a brain so that I may think for myself and make the world better?" She looks around the room. "We can bring about God's kingdom on earth only if we *all* are allowed to use the gifts God has given us. Women as well as men! And in a republic, that will mean the right to vote."

Doña Carmen clenches her hands and starts to speak, but more chanting drowns her out.

"Dignity! Respect! Liberty!"

"*España Libre, Mujeres Libres!* Liberated Spain! Liberated Women!"

The two Basque men beside me shake their heads and mutter.

Doña Carmen covers her face with her mantilla and storms out.

CHAPTER TEN

14 de abril, 1931
April 14, 1931

"**A**upa *Errepublika!* Long live the Republic!"

Father Itcea's spirits fell at the words spilling out of Bar Herria, yet his feet took him straight toward them.

That can't be! A republic would bring chaos. The Communists made only empty promises and blamed everyone else for their problems. Anarchists looked for any excuse to tear things down. Surely these men—his parishioners, whom he'd taken such pains to educate properly—wouldn't have fallen for their political tricks?

The bar was so crowded he could barely squeeze inside. "*Barkatu.* Excuse me." He nudged aside the villagers who usually cleared a path for him.

"We have won! We have won!" patrons cheered. "The king must go!"

"Wishful thinking," the priest said under his breath. Had the final returns from the election come in? He looked for a place to sit. Customers crowded the bar, even though many tables sat empty.

"Father Itcea!" Old Simon waved him toward the cash register.

As he made his way, the priest noticed the wallets and change purses on the bar, and he realized why everyone huddled here: only Bar Herria had both a radio and a telephone.

Old Simon gave his own barstool to Father Itcea and poured him a whiskey. The priest could not tell from the proprietor's demeanor whether he felt happy or unhappy with the possibility of a new republic. Father Itcea took a drink to steady his nerves. The smoky liquid burned his throat, though he did not protest when Old Simon poured him more.

"Shh, shh." Old Simon signaled to his clientele, his ear to the radio. "They're making an announcement!"

The patrons quieted down with a rapidity Father Itcea had never seen when similarly exhorted to silence during Mass. He took a drink, bracing himself for the news. The radio blared.

King Alfonso XIII, the last of the Bourbon dynasty, yielded his throne today. Spain is now a republic.

Ave Maria! Father Itcea felt as if he'd been kicked in the stomach. How could the people abandon their king?

Through the blackness of the moonless night, Alfonso left the palace by the garden gate and left Madrid before anyone was aware of it.

"The coward!" yelled the man to Father Itcea's right. Old Simon hushed him, then filled up the priest's glass.

His destination is being kept secret to ensure his safety. Unconfirmed reports indicate that he is on his way to Marseilles.

The priest took a swig; nips would not do for this terrible news. Old Simon filled his empty glass.

The Republic does not promise us happiness, but it will strive to bring back to Spain respect for law and justice.

Bring them back? Father Itcea gulped down his whiskey; his head spun. These people didn't know anything! A Spain unmoored from Christian beliefs—that would disrespect law and justice!

We are going to have peace and order above all else. What has happened today is a demonstration of the law-abiding nature of the Spanish people and should show our solid qualities to all those of the other nations with whom we seek to remain on friendly terms.

"Like France!" The man to his right lifted his glass and sang *"La Marseillaise"*:

Allons enfants de la patrie	Let's go children of the fatherland
Le Jour de gloire est arrivé!	The day of glory has arrived!
Contre nous de la tyrannie	Against us, tyranny's
L'étendard sanglant est levé!	Bloody flag is raised!

Other voices joined in. The men on either side of Father Itcea raised their fists. He drank deeply, the spirits coursing through his blood.

Entendez-vous dans les campagnes	In the countryside, do you hear
Mugir ce féroces soldats?	The roaring of those fierce soldiers?

More people joined in, more raised their fists. Father Itcea took a swig of his whiskey. Old Simon made his way smoothly down the bar, freshening the drinks.

Il viennent jusque dans nos bras	They come right into our arms
Égorger nos fils	To slit the throats of our sons
Nos compagnes!	Our comrades!

A young man drew a forefinger across his neck, his eyes round and droopy with drink. No fire of revolution burned there. Father Itcea recalled that even the most apolitical of people loved to sing this most militant of songs.

The man beside him downed his drink, then pounded on the bar, his rhythm the percussion that led into the refrain. Father Itcea raised his glass, ready to sing along.

"Why are we singing that for?" asked a man on the other side of the bar. "*Aupa Euskalerria!* Here's to a free Basque Country!" He slapped the back of the man singing "La Marseillaise" and burst out:

Gernikako arbola	The tree of Gernika
Da bedeinkatua	Is blessed
Euskaldunen artean	Among Basques
Guztiz maitatua	Absolutely loved

The customers, including Father Itcea, took each other by the shoulders and swayed to the tune. The priest held his drink as he sang along with his brethren.

Eman ta zabalzazu	Give and deliver
Munduan frutua	Fruit to the world
Adoratzen zaitugu	We adore you
Arbola saindua	Holy Tree

His vision blurring, Father Itcea thought about the Spain that he loved so much: unified under a king, obedient to the Church. Then he recalled a visit he'd made to Gernika as a young man, and how overwhelmed he'd been by this symbol of Basque independence.

Letting the emotion of the song envelop him, he sang at the top of his lungs.

Adoratzen zaitugu   We adore you
Arbola saindua!   Holy Tree

Old Simon led his patrons in enthusiastically singing the last word one more time, drawing out the last three notes: "*Saiin-duuuu-aaaaa.*"

The last word, *holy*, reminded Father Itcea of the other verses, which no one ever sang at a bar: the one asking God to bless the Basque Country with peace and strength, and the final verse, his favorite, thanking the Queen of Heaven for keeping the Basque Country free from war.

I should teach these people those verses!

He tried to remember the exact words, but the twelve verses jumbled together.

How do those verses go? Somewhere, he thought, they mentioned God and the old laws. That's what his people needed to hear about. Father Itcea put his head in his hands to concentrate. His cheeks felt warm and his head pounded; this brought him back to himself. He looked at the mirrored wall behind the bar, mortified at his reflection. Even at that distance, he could see his crimson cheeks and disheveled hair.

It would not do for a priest to be seen thus at a bar. He waved away the whiskey Old Simon offered him and stumbled toward the exit. Laughter filled the air: men vied with each other to buy drinks; women chatted as they waited for their turn at the phone; children kept singing along, even when they didn't know the words. Smiles brightened every face. Father Itcea had not seen these people in such good humor since he'd arrived in Indartze.

Let them enjoy themselves while they could. They did not know that only a country based on God's laws would last.

Blanca felt worried. Cruz hadn't returned from town where Ama and Aita had sent him to find out the election results. She feared her brother might get caught up in the violence. She had overheard whispers from her parents' hushed tones: "church burnings," "revolution," "demonstrations," "abdication."

It was just after sunrise. Her mother seemed unconcerned. She reminded Blanca how Cruz had come home safely after spending all night searching for that missing man, even when he'd braved going into the depths of the "witches' cave" alone to find him.

"God protected Cruz then," Ama had told Blanca. "God will protect him now."

Blanca knew it was the Blessed Mother who had kept Cruz safe. What was taking her brother so long to get home this time?

The tinny sound of a horn blaring and the crunching of wheels racing up the dirt road jolted Blanca from her seat.

"*Viva la libertad! Viva la República!*" Several voices yelled, honking a motorcar's horn, laughing.

Ama grabbed a hammer and moved to the window overlooking the front of the house. Blanca rushed to her mother's side.

"*To!*" Ama said. "Hey, look!"

Blanca looked out the window and couldn't believe what she saw—the fanciest motorcar she'd ever seen, black and shining in the morning sun. A sign across the door read "*Viva la República!*" The passengers stomped their feet, making the automobile shake. "We threw Alfonso out! We threw Alfonso out!"

Blanca remembered the Blessed Mother's message during her first visit: "The evildoers will soon engulf Spain."

The evildoers had come to her house!

The automobile door opened and out stepped her brother. The red band of the Republic on his sleeve, he waved a small red, purple, and yellow flag of the Republic. He closed the door behind him, then turned back and kissed a girl in the back seat.

Blanca gasped in recognition of the girl with the straw-colored hair and blue eyes.

The automobile sped away, leaving Blanca overwhelmed with questions: What was Cruz doing with that girl? Where did he meet these people with their fancy automobile? Would they get Cruz into trouble?

"Blanca," Ama said, "move away from that window." She tucked the hammer into her apron. As she made her way to the stairs leading to the front door, Ama crossed paths with Aita entering the kitchen. They touched hands and exchanged a look.

Blanca kept looking at the scene below, anxious to see what her mother would do.

Her father closed the shutters. "Do as your mother said." He gestured that she should move away from the window.

"Aita." Blanca sat beside her father. "What is happening?"

"I wish I knew." He took off his beret and rubbed his forehead. "Those people look like the *gaiztotzaileak*, those corruptors, Father Itcea has been warning us about."

Blanca's heart thumped. Father Itcea had been giving homilies for weeks on how bad things would be in Spain if the Republicans won. They would take people's land away. Burn churches. Make women work so that no one would be at home to take care of the children. God would be taken out of schools and everyone would go to hell.

"Aita?" She didn't dare look him in the eye. "I know you told me not to tell anyone, but . . . that time, on Aranzibia Hill . . . the Blessed Mother said this would happen. She said evildoers would come and would set Spain on fire. Fires as big as those of hell." Blanca closed her eyes, as she often did in the confessional, to give herself courage. "Then the Blessed Mother said I had to help her, that I needed to *gaizkatu herria*." It felt so good to finally ask her question: "What does *gaizkatu* mean, Aita?"

"That's a big word for a little girl. It means to 'exorcise' bad spirits, to 'liberate' someone or something from evil." Her father looked past her. "It also means that you have been chosen for a special mission."

Aita put her hands in his.

"Just like another young girl in our family many years ago." He sighed. "It's about time you learned about her. Her name was Maria."

Then Ama and Cruz walked in.

CHAPTER ELEVEN

The next morning Father Itcea's still-pounding head rendered his alarm clock unnecessary. It had been many, many years since he'd drunk so much, but he had only himself to blame. He took his time dressing as he recited his usual litany of morning prayers. The final phrase of the Act of Contrition called out for special attention: "O my God, I firmly resolve with the help of thy grace, to sin no more and to avoid the near occasions of sin. *I will not go to that bar again.* Amen."

He went directly to his office, forgoing breakfast as penance. He closed the door behind him, determined to compensate for last night's sins with good works today. There on his desk lay a thick envelope postmarked St. Jean Pied de Port. No doubt there had been the usual postelection trouble that followed the deposing of a king.

SPAIN'S STEADINESS AMAZES OBSERVER—by G.U.

The revolution in Spain is the most important single revolution from autocracy that has occurred in Europe. Spain has done the job with neatness, dispatch, and no casualties.

No casualties? Father Itcea did not wish violence on anyone, of course, but surely someone would have realized the mistake of expelling Alfonso and made their protest known?

The Republic is manifestly a decision of the people, calmly and uniquely expressed in municipal elections. One can say only that the Spanish people have shown a wisdom that is above all praise. After the joy and excitement, they have returned to work as if it were just a national holiday.

Father Itcea skimmed the rest of the article, looking for some indication that the Royalists had at least argued for some role for Alfonso. Wouldn't other world leaders, many of them his own relatives, demand as much? Only praise for the calm wisdom of the people filled these pages, except for one ominous note.

If a republic ushered in with such calm deliberation does not last, all the more reason for the economy of blood and thunder.

No one, least of all him, wanted this country to erupt in such chaos. But this caution was a good way to frame his homilies; he would emphasize that the peace of the Republic could be maintained only if it continued to follow the example of the Prince of Peace himself.

He jotted a note to remind himself of this point, then read on. Perhaps a dozen articles, all by the special correspondent G.U., relaying news along these lines. His stomach grumbling, Father Itcea looked at the clock; it would soon toll the noon hour. He would read one more article, then have an early lunch.

SPAIN TO NEGOTIATE SEPARATION OF CHURCH AND STATE
—by G.U.

"No, no, no!" Father Itcea took the newspaper to the window, in case he'd read the headline wrong. Alas, he had not.

Declarations by the Spanish Republic emphasized that there is absolutely no intention of confiscating Church properties were made today by the minister of the interior, Miguel Maura. He insisted, however, that there will be a separation of Church and state.

This is terrible! Father Itcea was glad he had fasted this morning, so he had nothing to vomit.

This will not be carried out with a high hand but will be arranged between the Holy See and this government with the interests of both considered, though this government will insist that the separation take place.

The government is not asking anything unreasonable, but merely the application in Spain of conditions already existing in other countries where Catholicism is widely practiced.

"*Ave Maria!*" Father Itcea slumped back into his chair. G.U. wrote as if those other Catholic countries were models for Spain to follow! Father Itcea had been to France. He'd seen the cesspools of immorality the cities had become without the Church to rein them in.

The barks of the neighborhood dogs shook Blanca awake. She threw on her housedress and coat and opened the shutters to see if she could see what the dogs were up to. The rays of the sun enveloped her mother, engaged in pruning her special "mystical roses." Among the few things her mother still had from her childhood home, they now stood almost as tall as Ama did. Blanca watched her mother, bending to cut a prickly stem, then carefully laying the pink blossom in a broad woven basket slung on her arm. After removing the thorns, she would put the roses in vases in each room, their blossoms brightening their home's plain décor.

"*Merde!* Shit!" Ama grimaced, putting her finger in her mouth.

"I'm coming, Ama!" Blanca darted down the stairs to get her work shoes. She almost ran into her father, catching his breath, his forehead sweating and his eyes watery. In his shaking hand he held a letter, ripped open.

"What's wrong, Aita?" Blanca took his arm.

"It's your grandmother Angeline." He sounded dazed. "She's dead."

"What happened?" Blanca settled her father into his kitchen chair before sitting herself down.

He shook his head. "*Ez dakinat.* I don't really know," he said. "Her neighbor Maria Jesus sent us this letter. She went to your grandmother's to take her to Lourdes for more holy water."

Blanca's temples pulsed. Didn't Amatxi need that water to keep her epilepsy at bay?

"She never made it," Aita said. "Maria Jesus found your grandmother all dressed up and ready to go. Then suddenly she stared blankly at her and said something odd in a voice Maria Jesus didn't recognize." His voice caught. "Then she fell down dead."

He handed Blanca the letter and added softly, "Her last words were for you."

Blanca skimmed through the letter, gasping at what Amatxi Angeline had said: "Blanca has the gift. She must use it."

I stumble down the stairs from my room and in to Bar Herria. Early morning works best for talking to tavern owners, I have found. I help Old Simon take down the upturned stools on the bar and greet him with the phrase I have heard used here.

"*Egin duzu lo?*" I set some coins down on the counter. "Did you sleep?"

He grins and prepares my coffee au lait. We listen to his favorite newscast, broadcast from Bayonne.

After dropping steadily for nearly a week, the peseta today reached its lowest point since the Spanish-American War. This led to a reaction on the Madrid and Barcelona exchanges, which deal mainly in local securities, bringing a sharp slump in prices and a pessimistic market.

A number of local and foreign bankers consulted today were unanimous in saying the present state of political uncertainty has played a large part in bringing the peseta to new lows.

Strikes in Andalusia have added to the distrust abroad. In Sevilla today, the strike was virtually over in Málaga. Some workers returned to work, but a general strike developed today at Granada, and workers at Córdoba are expected to join the farm laborers there who are already striking. All the ironmakers in a large metal plant in Bilbao are out, and a general strike has been called for Monday.

Old Simon turns down the volume and wipes the counter.

"Do you think a strike will be called here?" I ask.

"Who am I to say?" He shrugs. "We don't have any of those big factories. The workers around here seem pretty content."

Before lighting up my own cigarette, I offer him a Gaulois, which he waves aside. "The workers who came to that meeting here didn't seem happy."

"I've seen worse," he says. "And I've seen people on the other side just as riled up."

"Like Doña Carmen?" I take the opening, though I tread lightly whenever asking a man about his wife. "She seemed to be upset about what Sofia was saying."

"My wife is a staunch Catholic." Old Simon scrubs vigorously at a spot on the counter. "The strength of her convictions is more than enough for two." He puts his rag away; the counter now shines, spotless.

"It doesn't bother her that you don't go with her to Mass?" I ask.

"She knew what she was getting when we married," Old Simon says. "And I knew what I was getting. We respect each other's beliefs, and that's that." He grins. "Besides, it's good for business. The Catholics, the atheists, the monarchists, the radicals, they all love a drink."

The door opens and a pile of newspapers is placed on a counter inside. Old Simon unties the pile. I hope perhaps *Le Matin* has made its way here. Instead he hands me the local paper, *Gure Txoko*. Though most are written in Basque, some headlines in Castilian interest me. On the back pages I see a drawing of St. Michael the Archangel, sword in hand, a dismembered serpent at his feet. Basque words encircle the image.

"What does this say?" I ask.

"*Mikel Saindua Zaindu Euskal Herria*—Saint Michael, Protect the Basque Country," he says. "Then the article below it is titled '*Jaingoikoa eta Lege Zaharra*—God and the Old Laws.'"

"I've heard that phrase before." I snuff out my cigarette in the ashtray. "It refers to the *fueros*, the charters dating back to the Middle Ages, doesn't it?" Caireann had told me about these agreements, granting Basques some autonomy from the Crown in making their laws. "Do you mind translating it for me? The article likely will have interesting political opinions."

"Opinions, anyway," Old Simon mumbles to himself as he reads: "Against the new constitution. For letting secular authorities take over schools and cemeteries, among other things."

"Ah, does it say that without the guidance of the Catholic Church, all of society will fall apart?"

"More or less." Old Simon grins.

"The Church says the same thing in Ireland." I hold up my cup for the second helping Old Simon offers me.

"This writer feels strongly about that." He points to the middle of the article. "Here he says, 'The Church is above all political parties. We must supersede the politics that divide us, for only religion unites us.'"

I scoff at this line, and Old Simon raises a brow.

"And here, it says the Holy See obliges all Catholics to combat bad press and amplify good press," he says. "They recommend newspapers, especially, as ammunition par excellence for this purpose."

"As to the power of the press, I couldn't agree more," I say. "Tell me, Simon, do you read *Le Matin*?"

Sitting on the floor in Amatxi Angeline's bedroom, Blanca stretched out her legs underneath the open armoire. The hardwood floor felt cool and smooth. She breathed in the oak of the wardrobe and the pungent odor of mothballs. She touched her grandmother's clothes hanging there: a cream-colored, high-collared, satin dress with a lace veil embroidered with roses; a long black mantilla; a multi-colored silk shawl; a silk, velvet, and satin coat; frilly blouses over long, bell-shaped skirts; a fitted silk chiffon dress; gold painted leather shoes; a painted silk gauze fan with mother-of-pearl sticks; and gloves, scarves, and shawls of various shades and textures. Blanca had never seen her grandmother-that-was in these clothes, and they looked expensive. She must have saved them for special occasions.

These clothes were the only things left of her Amatxi Angeline, personal things that had caressed her grandmother's skin. Blanca wiped away a tear. If her mother could do this without crying, so could she.

"Blanca," Ama called from across the room, "come see if there's anything here you want."

Blanca rose, straightened her skirt, and wiped her cheeks dry. Her mother was taking items out from Amatxi's walnut trunk. Over Ama's arm dangled rosaries of many hues, and beneath these she carried monogrammed linens. Ama took out more linens, as well as letters and other documents. Then she took out a large book. Its thick yellow paper cover had big red letters at the top in French. The pen-and-ink etching below the letters terrified her, for it showed a huge goatlike monster towering over a young girl about Blanca's age sitting under a grove of four trees. The goat-monster stared right at Blanca. The girl sat naked at its feet but faced the other way, seeming not to even notice him.

"What is *that*?" asked Blanca, the hairs on the back of her neck prickling.

"I loved this book when I was young," Ama said, a faraway look in her eyes. "Its title is *Légendes et Récits Populaire du Pay Basque*—Legends and Popular Tales of the Basque Country—and it's by S. Elizalde. It's a collection of folktales my mother would read to me when she tucked me in at night."

Bedtime stories? Blanca wondered how stories in a book with a cover like that could make anyone want to go to sleep.

"The picture used to scare me, though the stories themselves aren't so frightening." Ama hugged Blanca. "This creature here"—she pointed to the goat-monster—"he's supposed to be the devil. And this young girl there, the devil's trying to get her into trouble." Her mother's eyes narrowed and she pursed her lips. "It's her own fault because she's tempting him by not wearing any clothes."

Blanca looked from the etching to her mother. That was a terrible story. How could this book be her mother's favorite?

"The girl eventually learns the error of her ways. She tricks the devil and gets away." Ama smiled. "I'll take the book home. You can read the stories to me in Basque and I will read them to you in French. It's how your Amatxi taught me. Would you like that?"

Ama had never offered to read with her before, or teach her French. The idea seemed to make Ama so happy, so Blanca nodded.

She looked more closely at the etching on the cover and shuddered: the grove the naked girl was sitting in looked exactly like the grove on Aranzibia Hill.

CHAPTER TWELVE

"**M**eow, meow!" Xuriko clawed at Blanca's bedroom door in the pitch dark, waking her. She tried to ignore Xuriko's pleas to open her door, but the kitten's meows got louder and her scratching more insistent.

Worried her cat would wake the whole family, Blanca peeled off her bedding, careful not to disturb Rosa, and put on her coat. She tiptoed to the door and opened it. Instead of coming inside her room, Xuriko bolted down the stairs toward the front door. Blanca turned on the flashlight from her coat pocket and followed her cat down the stairs, flinching with each creak of the floorboards. She opened the door, and Xuriko settled herself on the step, rubbing her nose against Blanca's shoes.

But Cruz's shoes were not at their usual place on the mat. *Where could he be?* It was too early for him to be milking the cows. She listened for stirrings from the barn below but heard nothing. Then she noticed a light moving through the darkness, on the path leading to town.

That must be him! Blanca put on her shoes, patted Xuriko's head, and followed the light. Where could Cruz be going so early in the morning?

Then she remembered: today was the first day of the Month of Mary! Maybe Cruz left for early morning Mass? She'd been praying for Cruz. He hadn't been to Mass for weeks. Now that her mother had started going again, he stayed home "to protect it." A cool breeze made Blanca shiver. In her hurry she hadn't finished buttoning up her coat and had forgotten her scarf. She tried to button the collar with her free hand, but her fingers stiffened with the cold. They fumbled and the flashlight fell to the ground. Birds flew up from the trees and cried out.

"Who's there?" Cruz shouted. "Why are you following me?" His flashlight moved quickly toward her, his footsteps stamping angrily over the brush.

"It's me!" Blanca yelled back. "Just me!"

"Stay there!" Cruz called out again, concern in his voice.

As she waited, Blanca wondered about her brother's tone.

The orange-pink of the coming day brightened the sky as Cruz reached her. "Well, it's too late to take you home. You'll have to come with me." He gave her his gloves and scarf and took her hand.

Blanca hoped Cruz would tell her what was going on. He trudged ahead, saying nothing.

"The Blessed Mother will be so happy!" Blanca said, to break the silence.

"What?" Cruz asked.

Blanca blushed. She hadn't told Cruz about her visions yet. "I meant, today we celebrate the Queen of Heaven. She would be happy that you're getting up so early to go to Mass."

Cruz grunted. "We're going to something more important than that."

Blanca could think of nothing more important than Mass for the Blessed Mother.

"Can you go faster?" Cruz asked. "We need to get to the plaza before the sun fully rises."

Blanca quickened her pace.

"Let's go!" Cruz winked at Blanca. "We don't want to miss the song!"

Oh, Blanca loved singing! This must be a special song if they had to get up so early to hear it. As they rounded the last bend into the plaza lit up with flashlights, she saw a huge crowd filled mostly with young people in work clothes. Many held the purple, yellow, and red flag Cruz had held when he came home in that fancy motorcar. Other people waved a red flag with a symbol on it that Blanca couldn't make out in the dim light. A song in Castilian wafted toward them from the plaza.

Arise, fellow-workers
For the day has dawned
It's the First of May
When the general strike is called!

Let's sing together
Of the glory of labor
For having thrown off
The yoke of slavery

Blanca didn't understand all the words, but the people sang them with such passion. She looked more closely at the men and women in the plaza: factory workers in overalls, farmers in the thick cotton garb they wore in the fields. Cruz tightened his grip on her hand, leading her through the crowd. A wooden platform had been raised there with a banner that read "Workers! Unite for Victory!" On the platform, leading the singing through a bullhorn, stood the blond girl Cruz had kissed.

Oh, no! Ama would not be happy about this!

Before the platform stood a phalanx of muscular young men, arms folded stiffly across their chests. They looked like the troublemakers who'd been in that automobile.

Cruz took her to the front row. "I have to go up there, sweetie. I'll come back for you later." He met her eyes. "Stay here with my friend till then." He turned to the boy next to her.

It was Refugio! The rays of the new day shone on his face: his hazel eyes sparkled, his chestnut curls peeked out from beneath his brimmed felt hat. His coat had patches at the elbows but otherwise looked in good shape. And he held himself with such confidence.

"You got here right on time!" Refugio said. "This is my favorite song!" He sang with the crowd, in Castilian.

Young workers, new proletarians
Come to us, come without fear . . .
We are the partisans of a noble cause
We are the advance guard of a better world

Cruz had made his way through the throng and stood with the other young men in front of the platform, his expression as severe as Father Itcea's when delivering a stern homily.

Our red flag will remain
The faithful symbol of its sacred mission
To lead the oppressed
To their liberation

Blanca had never seen so many people at one place at one time. Now that the sun had risen, she noticed children even younger than her were there. Some seemed to know all the lyrics. Others rocked back and forth, perched on their parents' shoulders. Young and old alike raised their fists when they finished the song, then repeated the last two lines, clapping along with the words. So many strangers, with so much enthusiasm. Yet Blanca did not feel afraid. She felt part of something bigger than herself. Something powerful.

"What do you think?" Refugio said. "I gather you've never been to a demonstration before. I remember being nervous the first time I went to one of these." Refugio took Blanca's hand. "Don't be frightened. These are all good people, trying to make a better world."

She let him hold her hand. She liked how it felt.

Father Itcea awoke with a start, hearing animated singing streaming in from the plaza.

Come, swell our ranks
Lend us a hand, be ready
For our fight is the cause of humanity
And will be long and hard to win

Just what he'd had feared! Once the king left, these radical outsiders moved in with their empty promises. Father Itcea had failed if his parishioners could not see through their godless bombast. Feeling heavy with sadness, he put on his robe, walked to his office, and opened the shutters to look out onto the plaza. He refused to hide from his people. He took in the scene outside, and his jaw dropped at the huge crowd. Men and women, even children, singing in unison, the mood as festive as a saint's day celebration. Instead of Indartze's banner, the Soviets' red flag with the yellow hammer and sickle presided over this gathering.

Socialism is our red banner
We will never let it fall
We will give our lives to hold it high
We will carry it to triumph

These predictions of triumph always got people into trouble. The demonstrators settled down as the young woman on the platform took up her megaphone to speak. She looked familiar.

"*Obradores!* Working people! A new day dawns in Euskal Herria!"

The protesters roared and waved the Communist flag.

This girl was no foreigner. She used the Basque term for "Basque Country" and pronounced the s like *sh* perfectly, something outsiders could never quite do.

"Today is the first official Day of the Worker, declared by our democratically elected government!"

More cheers rose from the gathering.

"The men and women of Spain have risen, inspired by a heroic, magnificent, and powerful urge. The Basque people look upon the world from the heights of the Pyrenees and proclaim in a loud voice, 'Long live the Democratic Republic!'"

"Long live the Democratic Republic!" The people chanted. "Long live the Democratic Republic!"

With a simple raising of her hand, the girl silenced them.

"Our voice is heard around the world. Our victory over tyranny is a victory for world democracy! The working people have spoken! The working people have been liberated from the yoke of 'divine' monarchy." The girl spat out the words. "We have found the strength to say, 'We can rule ourselves!'"

The throng took up the call: "We can rule ourselves! We can rule ourselves!"

The moment she lifted her megaphone, the horde fell silent.

Alarmed by the girl's power over the crowd, Father Itcea realized where he'd seen her before: she was the girl who had stopped the mob from hurting that *agota* boy.

"We working people, women and men, must devote all our efforts and minds to develop the prosperity of this country," the woman declared. "We will work for a new Spain: Where hard work is rewarded with honest pay! Where the pleas of the factory worker are heard as loudly as the demands of the factory owner! Where the value of women is equal to the value of men! Where the children of landless peasants are educated the same as the children of the landlord!"

The audience whooped at these words, yet the girl's insistent voice could still be heard: "We will have enough bread to eat! Our children will have enough milk to drink. Workers will reap the rewards of their own labor!"

"So-fi-a!" The throng took up the chant in waves. "So-fi-a! So-fi-a!"

Sofia raised her hand and quieted the assembly. "This day is not about me." Her tone turned sober. "Spain has had enough of following the dictates of individual leaders. We have been fooled too long to believe in the wisdom of the 'ordained' few." Her voice cracked and she lowered her megaphone. The gathering waited so quietly that Father Itcea could hear the chirping of the birds swirling overhead. "It is the wisdom of the working people that we must believe in now. Long live the people! *Aupa herria!*"

"Long live the people!" The demonstrators roared back, clapping and whistling in approval. "*Aupa herria!*"

Father Itcea felt caught up in the excitement. The tolling of the bells of Our Lady of Sorrows brought him back to himself. He closed the shutters and hurried to the sacristy to put on his vestments. Ordinarily he found this kind of talk against the ruling class dangerous, and he would move immediately to silence it. Yet he agreed with what she said about righting injustices against the poor. But this was God's work, not man's. And certainly not that girl's.

He took up his lectionary and looked over today's readings: Psalm 102, "Prayers of an Afflicted Man." It enjoined God to "respond to the prayers of the destitute" and praised those who did "deeds of justice."

The correspondence of Sofia's message with this psalm chilled him.

"Aupa herria! Long live the people!" Blanca chanted alongside Refugio, taking up the hand of the stranger on her other side.

How exciting!

"Aupa herria!" The multitude cried out in unison, the voices echoing off the walls of the handball court on the plaza, drowning out the tolling of the bells of Our Lady of Sorrows. As the chanting and pealing came to an end, a woman let out the *irrintzi*, the high-pitched Basque yodel-like cry of happiness. Two other women followed suit. Thunderous applause arose from the crowd. Blanca clapped along. She smiled so much her cheeks hurt.

"This is even better than the village festival!" she said to Refugio.

He looked at the ground. "Well, that wasn't very much fun for me."

Blanca felt her cheeks warm. What a stupid thing to say.

"I'm sorry." Blanca fumbled for the appropriate words. "I didn't mean—"

"—It's all right," responded Refugio. "Those people didn't know what they were doing. So much has changed since then."

How true. Since that festival, the Blessed Mother had told Blanca where the missing man was hiding, setting Refugio free from jail. She had discovered Aita secretly giving Refugio lessons, and now Refugio was helping her build a chapel for the Blessed Mother on Aranzibia Hill.

Cruz signaled to Blanca.

"Barkatu," she said to Refugio. "Excuse me."

As Blanca approached, Cruz held out his hand to Sofia.

Blanca stood in awe of her. Up close she saw flecks of violet in Sofia's eyes. The sun glinted off her hair as it bounced about her shoulders.

"Sofia," Cruz said, "you remember my sister, Blanca?"

The crowd circled around Sofia. The strong young men kept them at a distance.

"I'm so glad to meet you properly!" Sofia said in Basque. She kissed both Blanca's cheeks and gave her a warm hug. "Cruz has told me so many good things about you."

Sofia spoke softly. Such a contrast to her fiery speech on the platform.

Blanca lingered in Sofia's embrace, so warm and welcoming. Surely Ama would have no problems with Sofia if she got to know her.

"Let's have a seat." Sofia took Blanca's hand. "You have a long walk home."

Sofia sat Blanca down on a bench under the trees. Cruz remained standing, watching the crowd. "It's a beautiful day, isn't it?"

"Yes," Blanca said. *Just like the morning the Blessed Mother first appeared to me.* "A perfect beginning to the Month of Mary."

"I agree," Sofia said. "She was just a humble girl trying to heed God's call for her. Just like you and me."

Exactly what the Blessed Mother has been telling me! Sofia looked kindly into Blanca's eyes, waiting for a response.

"Sofia!" A drunken man stumbled toward them. "I love you!" Cruz led him away.

Sofia looked at Blanca with compassion. "Even people like him; he's probably just let the celebration go to his head. We all have our own wisdom and skills, even if it isn't always obvious. Did you know that's what *sofia* means, from the Greek, 'wisdom and skills'?"

Sofia's words amazed Blanca. "You know so much!"

Sofia laughed and squeezed Blanca's hand. "I've just had more chances to learn."

Blanca noticed the softness of Sofia's hand and the fairness of her skin. She had obviously never worked a day in the fields. "You are so lucky!" Blanca immediately felt guilty. "Not that I don't love my family."

"I understand," said Sofia, grinning.

Blanca blushed at the implication.

"All people, these people"—Sofia gestured toward the men and women milling about—"all of us are born with something special to offer the world, to make it better. Shouldn't all people have that opportunity, even if they're not born to money?"

"Yes," Blanca said. "I believe that with my whole heart!"

"It's good you feel free to say what you believe," Sofia said. "I wasn't brave enough to do that when I was your age. I hid my thoughts in a diary."

"I know exactly what you mean," Blanca said, proud that Sofia called her brave. "Only my doll Rosa knows what I really think!" It felt so good to share such thoughts and feelings with another person.

Sofia looked over Blanca's head. Blanca turned around and saw Cruz approaching. "We all have our own wisdom, our sense of what's right and true."

Sofia rose to greet Cruz. "We should listen to that instead of other people's foolishness."

Blanca sat, stunned. The Blessed Mother had used these same words.

Oh, Ama Maite Maria, she thought to herself, *do I betray you by thinking that?*

The church bells tolled eight. If she hurried, Blanca could catch the end of Mass and pray about it.

She rushed across the plaza toward Our Lady of Sorrows.

From my seat in the balcony, I see Father Itcea swing the thurible over the altar, as if to chase away the seeds of revolution Sofia has sown among the protesters outside. Though I have long been indifferent to the Feast of the Queen of Heaven, I followed the stream of people who came directly here from the protest. It seems incongruous that they would shout atheistic Communist mottos in one moment, then sing hymns the next. This would be an interesting issue to discuss in my next piece.

This Mass is in Basque, yet I recognize the tune from long ago. My lapsed religious beliefs aside, as a musician I still appreciate the beauty of the singing.

Aingeru batek Mariari	An angel said to Mary
Dio graziaz betea	You are full of grace
Jainkoaren semeari	To you the Son of God
Emanen diozu sortzea	Shall be born

The incense wafts up, taking the voices of the parishioners with it.

Agur Maria dena grazia	Hail Mary, full of grace
Miresgarria zoin ederra	A beautiful miracle
Gure bihotza hobenetarik	We offer the best of our hearts
Garbi garbia zuk begira	Pure and clean, to you

The incense stings my eyes, so I keep them closed. Without the visual stimuli, the singing enchants me.

Orduan berbo dibinoa	Then the divine word
Gorputz batez da beztitzen	Was made flesh
Oi, ontasun egiazkoa	Oh, true goodness
Jauna gurekin egoiten	For God to remain with us

I'm surprised to find tears on my cheeks and wipe them away. I open my eyes to take in parishioners as they sing the refrain:

Agur Maria dena grazia	Hail Mary, full of grace
Miresgarria zoin ederra	A beautiful miracle
Gure bihotza hobenetarik	We offer the best of our hearts
Garbi garbia zuk begira	Pure and clean, to you

They sing as if they believe its message, whatever it is, with all their might. I make a mental note of the protesters here. I cannot wait to talk to them about how they can sing this Marian hymn and chant Communist slogans with equal fervor. I imagine they all will gather at Bar Herria after Mass. By now I've mastered the art of insinuating myself among any company in that milieu.

The heavy iron door creaks open and men in the navy blue berets of the Spanish workers' parties come in. They stand in the side aisle by the back pews. The priest starts the last two lines again, perhaps to make the latecomers feel welcome.

Agur Maria dena grazia	Hail Mary, full of grace
Miresgarria zoin ederra	A beautiful miracle

In walks Sofia, flanked by Cruz and a little girl. It must be his sister, though they look nothing alike. Whereas the girl's black hair frames cherubic rosy cheeks and eyes as dark as the mythical black pools of Dublin, unkempt light brown hair spills out from under Cruz's cap.

Rays of the sun encircle Sofia's head. The men in the blue berets gesture that she should take a seat. Sofia waves the suggestion aside and harmonizes to the song from where she stands.

Gure bihotza hobenetarik	We offer the best of our hearts
Garbi garbia zuk begira	Pure and clean, to you

Her soprano rises sweetly over the melody and reverberates against the stone walls of Our Lady of Sorrows, echoing against the stained glass in the dome. The women in the front pews strain to reach her high notes; the men standing around Sofia pitch their voices to the melody of those in the pews.

The sound pierces my soul like a sword. The effect is beautiful, even ethereal. The last voice I heard this angelic was Caireann's. And my heart still aches whenever I think of her.

CHAPTER THIRTEEN

C hagrined at the memory of his last visit to Bar Herria, Father Itcea resolved to keep his composure this time. He adjusted his cassock and collar and opened the door. The Communist anthem "L'Internationale" immediately assaulted his ears:

Arriba, parias de la tierra	Arise, pariahs of the land
En pie, famélica legión	On your feet, starving masses
Atruena la razón en marcha	Reason deafens with its march
Es el fín de la opresíon	It's the end of oppression

The crowded bar had no room for the priest, but Old Simon acknowledged him as he busied himself pouring drinks.

Del pasado	Erase the trail of the past
Hay que hacer añicoa	It must be shattered
Arriba, esclavos, todos en pie!	Arise, slaves, on your feet!
Legión esclava en pie a vencer!	Slave legion, stand up to win!
El mundo va a caminar de base	The world will fundamentally change
Los nada de hoy todo han de ser	Today's nothings will be everything

Father Itcea had heard bursts of this song since his youth but made a point of not singing along. The refrain came next; he prepared himself for the exuberance and gesticulating that usually accompanied it.

Agrupémenos todos	Get together, everyone
En la lucha final!	In the final battle
El género humano	The human race
Es la internacional!	Is the international!

"Bertze bat, Eskuaraz!" a familiar voice called out. "One more time—in Basque!"

Ave Maria! Troublemakers had infiltrated his people after all!

Zutik lurrean kondenak	Arise, the condemned of the earth
Zaren langile tristea	The sad workers
Nekez ginen elkarganatu	We were worn down and fooled
Indazu albiristea	Proclaim the good news

Fewer patrons seemed to know these words, yet they all hummed along.

Gertatuak ez du ardura	What's happened has not worried us
Jende esklabua jeiki	Enslaved people, wake up!
Aldaketak datoz mundura	Changes are coming to the world
Nor den herriak badaki	It knows who its country is

Father Itcea scanned the crowd, looking for the man leading the singing. The customers took to their feet for the refrain, blocking his view.

Oro gudura ala!	Everyone, to fight!
Bihar izan dedin	So tomorrow we can be
Internazionala	An international
Pertsonaren adin!	People of reason!

Not all the words were pronounced right, suggesting that these Communists came from outside Indartze. This gave the priest hope. Those not native to these parts could more easily be rooted out. The crowd quieted down, returning to their drinks and conversation. Father Itcea noticed the *agota* boy Refugio. He hadn't seen him since his release from jail.

Then Father Itcea recalled he'd seen Refugio speaking to Sofia after her speech. He walked toward the boy, a strategy formulating in his mind.

"Good afternoon, Refugio." He held out his hand.

Refugio gave the priest a firm handshake. *"Berdin—*same to you, Father."

The priest noted that Refugio's clothes were fine, though his hands were calloused. He also noted that Refugio did not doff his hat, as was the custom when greeting priests.

And he could smell the whiskey on Refugio's breath.

"Can I get you a coffee?" Father Itcea signaled Old Simon before Refugio could protest. "It's good to see you doing so well."

"Thanks to you! That mob was going to kill me!" Refugio gestured in the general direction of the door, where the crowd had assaulted him.

"If I recall correctly, other people came to your aid that day as well. That boy Cruz ran across the plaza just in time." The priest pretended to search his memory. "That girl who spoke up . . .".

"Sofia," Refugio said. "She's wonderful!"

The worshipful tone in Refugio's voice would have bothered Father Itcea had he not been spellbound himself by Sofia's presence at Mass this morning.

"Sofia?" The priest feigned ignorance. "Is she the young woman who gave that speech in the plaza today?"

"Yes! She came to visit me in prison. I was all alone, no family, no friends. She brought me soup and bread to eat."

A sudden sense of guilt oppressed Father Itcea. He'd meant to visit the boy himself. He'd gotten distracted by all the newspaper articles Gabriel had sent, and he'd been busy composing those articles for *Gure Txoko*.

"She sounds like a fine young woman. I'm surprised I hadn't seen her before." He chose his words carefully so that Refugio wouldn't suspect he was looking into her. "Where is she from?"

"Bilbao," Refugio answered. "Her father owns factories there. She walked away from all that. She said her family had money only because they"—he looked up as though searching for the exact words—"'exploited the pro-le-tar-i-at.'"

Alarmed by these word, Father Itcea was filled with apprehension. This was classic Communist propaganda. He kept his expression neutral.

"She taught me to respect myself. She said it's not my fault I was born an *agota*. Even people like me have rights." Refugio pulled his shoulders back. "And all work has dignity."

That a girl from the aristocratic class would espouse such revolutionary views shocked Father Itcea. Private tutors had educated his own sister so that she would learn the values of the "perfect married lady," values appropriate to her station.

"Very interesting." The priest added sugar to his coffee.

"Sofia was the only daughter." Refugio took his coffee black. "She was supposed to marry the man her father had picked for her. Her brothers were sent away to private schools, though they spent most of their time gambling and hunting."

"I was undisciplined like that myself, before I entered the seminary." The priest couldn't help but smile. Although his father, abstemious to a fault, had rarely hosted parties himself, his wealth and royalist connections had put him and his relatives at the top of every prominent family's invitation list. Father Itcea had enjoyed these festivities immensely, feasting, drinking, and singing in the streets all night.

"Sofia went along with her parents when they decided she should marry her father's foreman," Refugio said. "He was the son of the owner of a nearby iron-works, though he wasn't going to inherit because he was not the oldest son."

The priest's skin prickled. This story sounded familiar.

"One day Sofia went to surprise him at lunchtime with his favorite potato-and-leek soup, which she'd made herself. . ."

Father Itcea choked on his coffee. He knew how this story ended: the girl goes to surprise her fiancé, only to find him and her father whipping the workers so hard their backs blistered with welts.

His mother had told him this story. About his youngest brother, Antonio, and his fiancée, Maria. Sofia must be her middle name.

Father Itcea returned to the rectory, anger and renewed grief overwhelming him. To think that this chit of girl had been responsible for his brother's death! After their rift, Antonio enlisted in the Moroccan war, where a bomb killed him. The priest had been informed that his brother's face had been blown off and his torso torn in two. The image still haunted him.

So did self-reproach. If only he'd provided better advice to Antonio, he might still be alive today. Father Itcea had blithely counseled his brother to consider a change of scenery. Given their father's wealth, Father Itcea assumed his brother would tour the Continent or retreat to the family's home in St. Jean de Luz. Too devastated to think straight, Antonio had instead thrown himself into a war for which he was utterly unprepared.

Eventually Father Itcea had comforted himself that his brother had gone to battle to prove himself to his true love. Now that he knew Antonio's fiancée was the radical Sofia, he burned with rage. For bewitching as she was, she was worth no such sacrifice.

"*Hator,*" Blanca's father said to her. "Come with me."

Blanca had just lit the day's first fire, surprised to see Aita up so early. Ordinarily Ama would wake him up, but she had returned to her family home to finish going through Amatxi Angeline's things.

"Don't worry about the fire," Aita said. "Cruz will be up soon to tend to it."

"*Bai*, Aita." Blanca rose to meet him. "Of course."

They walked in silence down past the "witches' cave," until they reached the path where the dirt road turned up toward Aranzibia Hill. Tiny leaves sprouted from the tree stump at the bend. Blanca offered to help her father sit on it, but he signaled her to sit there instead. He stood before her, resting on his walking stick.

"I've been meaning to tell you something." He looked past her. "Even though your mother wouldn't like it."

"I won't say a word," Blanca said.

"There's a good girl," he said. "I want you to know I believe what you told me, about the Blessed Mother appearing to you."

"*Esker mila*, Aita!" Blanca threw her arms around her father's waist. "Thank you!" Tears wet her cheeks. She hadn't realized until now how much she'd wanted her father to believe her.

"It's a story about another brave young woman in our family, who was also chosen for a special mission." Aita kissed the top of Blanca's head. "Your mother may be home soon, so I'm going to tell you the tale the quickest way I know how, the same way my mother told me, who learned it from her mother, and so on, all the way back four hundred years."

"Four hundred years?" Blanca said, shocked. What could a simple family like hers have done worth talking about after so much time?

Aita cleared his throat and sang, his voice shaky.

Jende onak, huna gu, huna gu	Good people, in this
Kantatu nahi dugu	We would like to sing
Egi zuzena beti aitortu	To proclaim the truth
Saindu Mariaren kondu	Of sainted Maria's story
Indartzen sortu eta hazia	Born and raised in Indartze
Indartsu zaiku Maria	Maria grew strong
Neska on ona, zoragarria	A good and wonderful girl
Bedeinkatzen gaituena	She blesses us

Where had Blanca heard this tune before?

Indartze ahultzera etorri da	To weaken Indartze came
Bakearen etsaia	The enemy of peace
Feliz Zigor gizon faltsua	The deceitful Feliz Zigor
Jendea sorgintzera	To bewitch the people

The song about the torture of Santa Agata! With different words. What horrible story would they tell?

The crickets beckoned Blanca from her sleep. She made her way slowly to the bedroom window so that the wooden floorboards would make as little noise as possible. She looked up at the clear sky full of stars. The full moon shimmered over the hills dusted with snow. She took a deep breath. She loved the feel of the cool air in her lungs.

It was quiet except for the crickets. Blanca closed her eyes, taking pleasure in the peace she felt all around her. Xuriko's meow startled her eyes awake.

"*Zer dion?*" Blanca brought the cat in from the roof connecting her room to the kitchen. "What are you doing there?"

The kitten purred against Blanca's chest and nudged her nose into her hand. Blanca loved it when she did that. Then she noticed that Xuriko's whiskers were wet with milk.

How strange, Blanca thought. *Who would be feeding her in the middle of the night?*

Putting the cat on the bed, Blanca slowly lifted the latch on her bedroom door. The door to the kitchen stood ajar, the glow of candlelight reflecting on the polished floorboards. She took the few steps toward the kitchen and peeked in, unobserved. And there she saw her mother, her long brown hair loose about her shoulders, wiping her tears with the sleeves of her white nightgown.

"Ama," her mother said between sobs, "how could you keep these from me?" She took a sip from the special glass she used for her tonic.

Then Blanca noticed the neatly folded pieces of paper strewn on the table, sticking out of envelopes or lying flat under the stones her mother used as paperweights. Blanca squinted. Some had handwritten letters on them, but others showed the even printed lines of newspaper articles. Her mother fished among the papers and held something up to the candle. It was a photograph. Blanca couldn't see it very well from so far away, but it looked like a picture of her mother as a young woman, holding hands with a man other than her father. The man in the photo was not round and short like Aita.

"You didn't abandon me after all!" Ama said.

Blanca's jaw dropped and she covered her mouth. She ducked her head behind the door, praying her mother hadn't seen her.

CHAPTER FOURTEEN

The late afternoon breeze cooling his back, Father Itcea sat on the wooden benches near the handball court, a newspaper tucked under his arm. He needed fresh air after spending so much time in his office, poring over the documents Gabriel had sent him.

Cruz played *mano-a-mano* against the *agota* boy, Refugio. Though Cruz was taller and older, Refugio was stockier and held his own. The score was even at twenty-eight, only two points away for a win.

In addition to reading Gabriel's correspondence and the reports of the visions at Lourdes, Father Itcea had studied Father Zabaleta, the seventeenth-century rector of Our Lady of Sorrows. This priest had single-handedly put a stop to the vigilantism against "witches" the ignorant villagers had conjured up in their midst. He felt confident he could weave these seemingly disparate narratives into a coherent argument about how Catholicism had tamed the obstreperous instincts of rural cultures like that of the Basques.

"If it weren't for Father Zabaleta's theological knowledge and pastoral skill," Father Itcea would write for his next installment in *Jaungoikoa eta Lege Zaharra*, "the whole village would have been convulsed in flames. Many innocent people would have been murdered, and many more would have died in the resulting violence." He hoped his articles would be enough to counter the anticlerical sentiments he overheard as he went about his day.

"*Jo!* Serve!" Refugio bounced the ball and struck it against the smoothed stone wall.

The priest watched the boys rally. At their age, he used to play *pilota* most afternoons. Never any good, he'd enjoyed the camaraderie and competition with his friends. The constant contact of the solid ball against his hands bruised and swelled his palms and fingers. Though he never got used to how much it hurt, he learned to hide the pain.

He unfolded the paper. Only newsprint and the occasional papercut marred his hands these days.

"Twenty-nine to twenty-eight." Cruz shouted the score as he served.

"*Hori!* That's it!" Father Itcea didn't care who won, but he remembered how he had liked it when onlookers reacted.

He laid the paper on his knees so that he could keep an eye on the game while reading *Le Matin*. The headline almost made him fall off the bench.

CHURCHES LOOTED. REPUBLICANS SUSPECTED—by G.U.

"*Mierda!* Shit!" Father Itcea said.

"I'm trying." Refugio looked at the priest sheepishly. He fetched the ball he'd missed, for Cruz to serve.

"Do your best, son." Father Itcea adjusted his spectacles and brought the newspaper closer to his eyes.

At least a half dozen persons were wounded today when soldiers fired into groups attempting to loot churches or burn other Catholic property. Three persons, carrying incendiary bombs, were arrested, and it was believed that similar bombs were used during the riots yesterday to set fire to buildings.

Ave Maria! Father Itcea crossed himself. *I knew this would happen!*

"*Jo!*" Cruz served. "Twenty-one to twenty-one!"

Two dozen church buildings were completely destroyed by fire, and perhaps ten more badly damaged but not burned. Nuns in almost every instance were respected by the crowds. Several monks and priests were beaten, but there were remarkably few casualties among them.

"Remarkably few?" The priest grumbled under his breath. "Even one is too many!"

"*Aire!* Airball!" Refugio backpedaled. He took a swing with his weaker, right hand, grimacing but keeping the ball in play.

Efforts to estimate the physical damage were mere guesswork, but some calculated that as much as 150,000,000 pesetas worth of damage had been wrought. Police arrested several looters on whom they found gold and silver altar ornaments, chalices, and candelabras taken from the churches.

Folding the paper, Father Itcea walked briskly to the rectory. He recalled the reverence with which Father Zabaleta had described the liturgical objects of

Our Lady of Sorrows. Father Itcea had not seen these sacred items, likely sequestered in a vault or safe somewhere in the vestry. These were precisely the kind of hallowed items godless vandals would love to melt down and sell on the black market.

He vowed to find them before they did.

"You may look now," Refugio said.

Blanca took her hands from her eyes and stood agape at what she saw: a cross in the middle of the grove! On top of it dangled a wreath of roses.

"It looks like the May pole!" Blanca giggled. "So festive!"

"It's not *too* festive, is it?" Refugio blushed. "I wanted it to feel welcoming to the weary, like the Blessed Mother said. Not look like a playground."

"It's lovely," Blanca said.

"I thought she might like the roses," Refugio explained, "since they decorated the veil she wore when she appeared to you."

He is such a good listener. Blanca didn't even remember telling Refugio about the Blessed Mother's veil.

The sun dipped overhead, but they had a few hours before it set. "What can I do to help?" Blanca asked.

Refugio seemed surprised by the offer. "I want to finish digging out a rock for the altar top. I could use some help with that, though I wouldn't want you to get your dress dirty. We could explain things to your father, but what would your mother say?"

Blanca considered the question. Ama had been much nicer since Amatxi Angeline had died, though she still chided Blanca when she did not look proper.

"I could sit on this." Blanca removed the extra apron she had put on to collect mushrooms. The memory of Blanca's first vision came to her, when she'd looked for the king of the mushrooms. How clever the Blessed Mother had been to visit Blanca while she went about her day.

"That sounds good." Refugio walked to a spot near the tallest and straightest of the four oaks, where a shovel lay. "There seems to be a slab we could use in here. Perfect for an altar: rectangular, its long side is about two arms' length across. I uncovered most of it with my shovel. I will dig out the rest with my hands so that I don't break it." He squatted down. "Can you help me?"

Blanca peered into the hole. The rock looked like a block made by a skilled stoneworker.

"I will try my best." Blanca took off her apron. Refugio laid it on the ground and reached out for her hand.

Blanca didn't need the help, but she took his hand anyway.

Refugio sat on the ground beside her and they dug in silence. A white-tailed eagle soared above them, its whistle echoing on Aranzibia Hill. Then another eagle joined it. Blanca smiled at how much they seemed to have to say to each other. She peeked at Refugio. He smiled back.

They dug like this, in silence except for the calls of the birds, and Blanca lost track of time. They had made a lot of progress in uncovering the rock, yet it seemed as if they had just started digging. Then a northern wind rustled through the grove, and the tallest tree dropped an acorn into the cavity.

Blanca reached in. "The acorn has fallen down the hole and is caught under a corner of the rock."

"It shouldn't take much effort to get it out," declared Refugio, who lay on his stomach so that he could reach farther into the hole, and Blanca did the same. "The slab looks man-made. It has level edges like someone carved it out, then put it here."

"Maybe it belonged to an old church?" Blanca's spirit soared. *How exciting that would be!*

"That could be why the Blessed Mother told you to build the chapel here," Refugio said.

Blanca dug her nails under the edge the acorn had struck and pulled. "It's giving way!" she exclaimed, amazed she had the strength to dislodge the stone.

Refugio placed his hands next to hers, and they pulled and pulled on the block. The eagles circled above them, calling out encouragement.

"Here it comes!" Blanca and Refugio said together. They heaved up the rock.

"Look!" Blanca said. "It has letters on it!"

"Here." Refugio removed the kerchief from his neck. "Use this to take the dirt off."

"I can read it now," Blanca said.

"What does it say?" Refugio pointed to the setting sun. "I can't read it."

"I can barely make out the words." Blanca neared the rock so that it almost touched her nose. "It says . . ." Refugio listened intently as she read aloud:

Sabineri,	To Sabine,
Etxeberria	A new house
Bizi berria	A new life
—*Indartzetarrak*	—The people of Indartze

"Who's Sabine?" Refugio asked.

"I have no idea." Blanca hoped her disappointment didn't show. Why would the Blessed Mother want a chapel built here?

On his hands and knees, Father Itcea searched for a secret opening or false door underneath the cabinet in the vestry. He had been up all night looking for the sacred objects Father Zabeleta had mentioned in his diaries, so that he could hide them. The sacristy would be the first place looters would look, and no doubt they would be as dogged in their search as he.

He had found nothing unusual in the cabinet thus far. He removed the ciborium that kept the Eucharistic host and the chalice for the wine and placed them on a small table beside the other items. He had shuttered the window to prevent late-night passersby from observing him, and his eyes felt strained from searching by candlelight. The flame shimmered on the plated gold of the ciborium and chalice; the makers' marks indicated their provenance to be the turn of the twentieth century. Other items appeared even more recently made: the candles for the altar and sconces, the missals and songbooks.

None of these objects would tempt pillagers. The ciborium and chalice would yield few pesetas if melted down, the candlestick and altar cards even fewer. But his mouth watered at the thought of the sixteenth-century sacred objects Father Zabaleta had described: the silver-gilt paten and chalice (What a joy to serve the Body and Blood of Christ from these!); the delicately carved ciborium; the jewel-encrusted monstrance for displaying the sacramental bread. The Communists and Anarchists could sell them on the black market for a high price indeed and with the proceeds fund innumerable attacks against Church property. That thought sent a shiver down Father Itcea's spine.

He rolled up his sleeves and readied himself to take a closer look.

"Ki-ki-ri-ki!" A rooster crowed.

Dawn already? The priest peered through the shutters. There perched the rooster on the water fountain. Its feathers puffed out, all bombast until a figure rounding the corner frightened it away.

"William's heading my way!" Father Itcea couldn't risk the fiddler seeing the rectory in such disarray and discovering his mission. He buttoned up his sleeves and hurriedly put on his cassock; it would cover the dust and dirt on his clothes. He passed a rag over his shoes; scuffs on morning footwear might suggest a night spent carousing.

He closed the shutters and cabinet door; he would continue his search later. Fortunately, no one else had the key to this room. He left through the church's side exit, near the outline of the *agota* door. He reached the plaza just as William approached the rectory, fiddle case in hand and a cigarette at his lips.

"*Bon jour*, William!" Father Itcea tried to sound buoyant. "Good to see you!"

"Good morning," William said.

The fiddler's rumpled shirt, wrinkled pants, and dust-coated shoes indicated an inauspicious beginning to his day. His long hair looked more unruly than usual, and dark circles shadowed his eyes.

"Off to an early start, I see," Father Itcea said.

"In a manner of speaking." William snuffed out his cigarette. "I learned a new word that captures it: *gau-pasa*."

Ah—the "all-nighter" of drunken revelry. That would explain the dusty shoes; the sawdust at the bar protected the wood floors from splattered drinks.

"I am on my morning stroll," Father Itcea said. "Have a good day."

"You as well." William waited for Father Itcea to pass, a deference the priest always appreciated.

Father Itcea walked briskly to the bookshop to buy his daily paper. He might even have time for a cup of coffee to perk himself up.

Le Matin's headline alone jolted him:

MOVE TO TRY KING ALFONSO FOR STAGING ANTI-MONARCHIST RIOTS—by G.U.

The priest kept walking to clear his head. He could not believe, refused to believe, what he'd read. If Alfonso instigated the violence, then he had put his trust in a king to whom human life meant nothing. Whose faith was false. If true, and the priest would find out for certain, then he had blamed the wrong people for all the mayhem. He exited the rectory and went down the cobbled road that led to the trail toward the botanical garden in the neighboring town. He'd heard it was beautiful.

An elderly gentleman walking by stopped and took off his bowler hat. "Good afternoon, Father."

"*Berdin*—same to you." Father Itcea quickened his pace so that the man would not expect a conversation.

The priest knew he should always engage in *cura personalis*—the "care for whole person"—of all he encountered, yet bigger concerns preoccupied him. Could he have been so wrong about Alfonso? Had he misplaced his loyalty to the Spanish Crown?

A young couple approached him on the road; the mother pushed a baby carriage and the father held the hand of a lively toddler.

"What a lovely family you have." Father Itcea forced himself to greet them. He should behave in a manner reflective of his vocation, no matter his personal circumstances.

"Thank you, Padre!" He heard the man call back.

They must be from out of town or they would have used his Basque title. Father Itcea wondered whether they had visited the gardens.

He took off his biretta and wiped the perspiration off his face. The sun bore down; fortunately, a breeze from the north cooled him. The roar of a waterfall suggested he was nearing his destination. Father Itcea walked through the wrought iron gates and fell in line with the crowds ascending the path up the cliff.

"Good day, Aita Itcea," said a woman. Probably a parishioner.

The roar of cascading water beckoned him, but Father Itcea did not want to seem harried in case other parishioners saw him. The hum of conversation around him suggested that many foreigners visited. He caught snatches of Castilian, French, and Catalan as well as the sonorous Basque dialects from across the border.

He mopped the sweat from his face. He hadn't expected this incline, and it'd been years since he'd done such a hike. The queue ahead of him slowed, so Father Itcea knew he approached the hilltop. An elderly couple rested on a bench under a thick-trunked yew with large branches festooned with leaves. Farther up, a young man sketched on an easel. Father Itcea avoided glancing at the drawing, for he wanted to experience the falls from a place of purity.

"Ze' ederra! How beautiful!" exclaimed several boys on their way down. The roar of the falls swallowed the rest of their conversation.

A silence descended on the crowd as it neared the clifftop. Only the whistling of the white-tailed eagles punctuated the quiet.

And a peace came upon Father Itcea too.

"Be still, and know that I am God." The phrase from Psalm 46 came unbidden, though not unwelcome: he often meditated on this phrase during his spiritual exercises.

No more sweat on his brow, no worries on his mind, the priest took the hand of the person ahead of him and held out the other to the person behind. Without speaking, everyone had formed a human chain to help one another ascend.

The priest reached the clifftop and stood in awe. The waterfall cascaded into a lake of turquoise beauty. In its still waters were reflected the beeches and oaks surrounding it and the ravens soaring overhead.

Consider the ravens. Father Itcea appreciated this reminder of the verse from Luke, chapter 12. *They do not sow or reap, they have no storeroom or barn; yet God feeds them. And how much more valuable are you than birds!*

He closed his eyes and said a prayer of gratitude for the calm he now felt. He need not worry about the king or the supposed monarchist plot. In the words of a mystic whose name he did not recall: "All shall be well, and all shall be well, and all manner of thing shall be well."

Father Itcea put on his biretta and made his way back to Indartze at a leisurely pace. He greeted the people he encountered along the way, chatting with those who seemed amenable. The gardens' fame had enticed people from as far away as Barcelona; one couple had come all the way from Paris.

The bells at Our Lady of Sorrows tolled.

He remembered the state of disarray in which he'd left the vestry and walked faster.

Ad maiorem Dei gloriam. The beautiful items Father Zabelata had described were made "for the greater glory of God." Like the falls, they should be enjoyed by everyone. They would bring people together and closer to God. He would talk to the boy Refugio about making a secure display for the valuable Eucharistic objects. *Agotas* were handy with tools. And the boy could likely use the wages.

Father Itcea reached Our Lady of Sorrows as the clock chimed seven. He would forego his evening meal, determined to find the items this time. He took the key from the ring at his waist and let himself in through the side entrance by the *agota* door.

He looked at the sacristy door in horror: "Noooo!" The lock was broken!

He rushed inside: all the ecclesiastic items were gone! In rising panic, Father Itcea ran to the altar: the statue of Our Lady of Sorrows had been decapitated, a hole punched through its bosom.

He collapsed onto his knees and wept.

CHAPTER FIFTEEN

The eyes of the peasant Christ on the rectory crucifix entreats me as I wait for Father Itcea. The grandfather clock chimes eight o'clock. The door to the priest's office opens and I rise. The priest escorts Doña Carmen out. The electric chandelier illuminates the Unión Patriótica brooch on her black silk blouse, inscribed with their motto *España Unida y Católica.*

"I'll send my girl over with the crystal decanter and silver bowl right away," Doña Carmen says as the priest walks her briskly to the door. "We won't let those dirty *agotas* get away with this."

"Now, now." Father Itcea extends his hand to me. "Let's not rush to judgment. We don't know who did this yet. The most important thing is to continue ministering to the spirit of the people regardless of the materials at hand. In the meantime, thank you again for your donation."

After ushering Doña Carmen outside, Father Itcea walks back to his office, indicating I should follow.

"She's pious and generous." He takes his seat and I take mine. "And I'm sure she means well, but we Basques hold fast to our stereotypes."

"Well, if it's any comfort, people cling to stereotypes wherever I go," I say. "As a roving fiddler, I am mistaken for a 'dirty gypsy' all the time."

The priest blushes. "What brings you here this evening, William?"

"I wanted to express how sorry I am about the robbery."

He smiles. "I'm surprised you would mind the loss, as I don't see you at Mass often."

He states the fact without judgment.

"I'm as itinerant a Mass-goer as I am a fiddler. I enjoy the music and ritual. It's the theology these days I take issue with. Too mean spirited for my taste." I shift in my seat. "Present company excluded, I'm sure."

"Unfortunately," the priest says, "many villagers attend Mass too infrequently to know."

"Oh, the Church means more to them than you might realize," I say. "I was in Bar Herria when the news broke. And the men were outraged. Is it true the thieves took the urn holding the ashes of Maria Gurrutxetegia, the accused witch burned at the stake in 1610?"

"It appears so." Father Itcea's voice broke. "And now I will be unable to continue my case for her sainthood. The people here, as you know, have been praying on her ashes for centuries, and healings have been rumored. Some villagers even encased Maria's remains in small religious objects they pass from home to home to pray over. However, we can independently test for the miraculous properties of the ashes only in their unadulterated form. And now they're gone."

"I had no idea!" I don't believe in miracles or the magical properties of ashes, but it seems an unkind thing to mention at this moment. "Why would the burglars want her ashes?"

The priest throws up his hands. "Who knows? They may not know what they have. They may have been after the vessels themselves. They also took other religious objects, sixteenth-century objects encrusted with valuable jewels." He pointed to the newspapers on his desk. "They likely will melt the items down to sell."

"Do you have any idea who the thieves might be?" I ask.

"The objects were sequestered inside the statue of Our Lady," he says. "It wouldn't have occurred to me to look there. So it has to be someone familiar with the church and its history, like a sacristan or an altar boy." He sighs. "A disaffected one, obviously."

"Obviously," I say. But the ashes could also have been taken by someone to whom the martyr's ashes meant so much. Perhaps they no longer trusted a Church in turmoil to keep them safe.

Grasping his black Lourdes rosary, Father Itcea prayed the Virgin Mary would give him the strength to finish the Mass said in her Son's name without betraying his inner turmoil. Likely the culprit who stole the objects from Our Lady of Sorrows, or a relative, sat in the congregation. Father Itcea approached the pulpit.

"A reading from the Book of Luke." He made the sign of the cross. "Chapter 23, verses 33 to 43."

Father Itcea's thoughts raced. *It's the story of the Good Thief!*

When they came to the place called the Skull, they crucified him and the criminals there, one on his right and the other on his left.

He made sure to enunciate the Basque word for "criminal"—*gaizkiletaria*, "one who does wrong."

One of the criminals who was hanged railed at him, saying, "Are you not the Christ? Save yourself and us!" The other rebuked him, saying, "Do you not fear God? For we deserve to be condemned for our misdeeds; but this man has done nothing wrong." And he said, "Jesus, remember me when you come into your kingdom." And he said to him, "Truly, I say to you, today you will be with me in Paradise."

Father Itcea held the book aloft. "This is the Word of the Lord!" His voice reverberated against the dome.

"Thanks be to God." The parishioners sat down.

Usually Father Itcea remained at the pulpit and read a prepared homily word for word. Today he moved away from the lectern and took the step down from the sanctuary, standing only a meter from the first row of pews.

"This Gospel speaks to the undying capacity of Our Lord Jesus Christ to forgive all of us sinners, for all of us do wrong." He preached without notes. "Even me."

This elicited a giggle from a child; Father Itcea ignored it. Mostly widows, young mothers, and small children attended weekday Masses. He would deliver his homily anyway, for these women had a way of passing along the Word of God to their families.

"This reading is usually known as 'The Good Thief.' A more accurate understanding would be 'The Penitent Thief.'" He stepped closer to the pews. "Because Jesus knew the Good Thief was sincere in his contrition, he welcomed him into Paradise."

"*Baietz!*" A girl's voice cried out. "Yes, indeed!" Father Itcea felt glad someone heeded his message.

"In this sense the Penitent Thief is an example to us all; if we are truly sorry for our wrongdoing, no matter how grave, God will forgive us and welcome us to His kingdom, through His Son, Jesus Christ."

The priest looked at the parishioners, hoping to see the power of his words reflected on their faces. Many had closed their eyes, as he often did when deep in prayer. He feared perhaps they had fallen asleep.

What more can I say to reach these people?

"Hail Mary, full of grace . . ." An elderly woman craned her head toward him. Practically deaf, she prayed the Rosary incessantly during Mass. Though she tried to keep her voice down, he could still hear her recitation: ". . . Pray for us sinners . . ."

This gave Father Itcea an idea.

"We are all sinners." He paced slowly through the aisle. "We sin because we feel separated from God. In the story of the Penitent Thief, God urges us to turn back toward him and away from sin. The Greeks have a word for this idea: *metanoia*."

The priest himself felt uplifted at these words, which seemed to come through rather than from him.

"As you know, Our Lady of Sorrows has also suffered at the hands of thieves." He gestured toward the altar. "They broke into this sacred church and desecrated the image of Our Lady, who has protected this church for centuries! They kicked her head off and stole the silver ciborium that stores the consecrated Body of Christ!" Father Itcea raised his voice. "The silver patens that hold the host during the Eucharist!"

His parishioners cried out, then hushed each other.

"They took the silver chalice that stored the sacramental wine." Father Itcea held up his hands to quiet the murmurings. "They desecrated our spiritual legacy by stealing the precious items hidden inside the statue for hundreds of years. That held the ashes of our beloved Maria Gurrutxetegia!"

Some worshippers choked back tears; others merely repeated the items he mentioned, as if to call them back.

"Even as Jesus was being crucified," Father Itcea said, "he asked his father to forgive the crowd that mocked him, saying, 'They know not what they do.'"

"*Baietz, Jauna!* Yes, Lord!" The little girl again.

"Perhaps the thieves did not know the significance of these sacred objects to the people of Indartze. Perhaps they thought only of the monetary gains they could reap by selling them, not the spiritual harm they would do by taking them."

The church was so quiet. Father Itcea felt sure everyone could hear his heart beating.

"Yet the Gospel today assures us even a thief can attain salvation, so long as he is penitent. The thief who confesses his sins and vows to sin no more will be forgiven by God and welcomed into heaven."

The priest walked back to the pulpit, where he kept his pocket calendar as well as the lectionary.

"This Sunday we will celebrate Pentecost, which commemorates the descent of the Holy Spirit upon Jesus's followers." He recited from memory the relevant words: "And suddenly there came from the sky a noise like a strong driving wind . . . and they began to speak in different tongues, as the Spirit enabled them to proclaim."

From the balcony, someone stifled a cough.

"For this reason, Pentecost is seen as the birthday of the Catholic Church. For the first time the apostles and believers—united by a common tongue—could go forth and preach the Gospel. Let us prepare ourselves for this holy feast by purifying our souls. I shall hold confessions for one hour before each afternoon Mass, beginning at four o'clock today, for all of you who would like to unburden yourselves of your sins." He gestured toward the altar. "However great or small."

He gripped the lectionary and looked sternly at the parishioners, even the unseen person in the balcony.

If you are the thief—he hoped they understood—*now would be the time to confess.*

The parishioners squirmed. The priest gestured that the congregation should rise for the closing prayers and final sign of the cross.

Customarily, priests did not process out with the parishioners after a weekday Mass, so Father Itcea turned around to blow out the candles on the altar as the parishioners exited. Normally, they lingered in the aisle to chat with each other or gathered in the back of the church to gossip. Today, only quick footsteps pinging the marble floor punctuated the solemn silence in Our Lady of Sorrows.

Father Itcea turned around to place Doña Carmen's crystal decanter and silver bowl in the tabernacle. He regarded the empty church. Not even the most pious of his parishioners had dared to engage him in conversation after Mass. He walked back to the pulpit to retrieve the lectionary and return it to the sacristy. Clearly, his homily had been effective.

A loud thud echoed from the church entrance, as if a large sack of grain had been thrown down.

Someone was up to no good.

Father Itcea grabbed a heavy candlestick from the altar and ran toward the sound.

"Blanca!" The girl's face was as white as the Eucharistic host. "Are you ill?" He crouched near the girl, letting the candlestick slip to the floor. She lay so still, her eyes staring blankly, and his hands trembled. *Is she dead?* He patted her cheeks gently: no response. He bowed down and turned his ear to her lips; thank God she was still breathing. Shallow, uneven breaths, but signs of life all the same. Father Itcea regretted that his homily had scared everyone off, for surely one of the women would know what to do.

The rosary fell out of his pocket as Father Itcea closed his eyes and made a quick plea to the Virgin Mary that she should guide him now.

When he opened his eyes, Blanca still lay on the floor, now with her arms outstretched as if hanging on a cross. The morning sun shone on her face through the stained-glass window of Hildegard von Bingen, the twelfth-century mystic. Blanca's face was so transformed as to become exquisite, something Father Itcea could not describe.

"Blanca," he said, "it's Aita Itcea. It seems you have taken a fall. Are you all right? Can you hear me?"

She muttered something, and Father Itcea thanked God that she seemed to be returning to normal.

What happened next was anything but normal.

"The king will bring salvation," intoned Blanca, her voice low and gravelly. Her eyes stared at a point over Father Itcea's head.

"What was that, Blanca?" Father Itcea drew his ear closer to her lips. He must have heard her wrong.

"The Bourbon king will save Spain!" Blanca clenched her hands. The specificity of the girl's statement captured the priest's attention. Until the recent elections, the Bourbon dynasty had ruled Spain for centuries. She could not know that on her own.

"Alfonso will return?" Father Itcea clasped his hands; his prayers would be answered!

"One day the king will return to Spain as the symbol of unity and permanence," Blanca said.

Father Itcea could barely contain his excitement. "When, my child?"

"The king will save Spain," Blanca continued to intone.

Clearly in an abstracted state, she did not sound like herself. What an honor for him to bear witness to these prophecies!

"He will face down the rebels who would wrest his crown from him," she continued. "He will bring the righteous together!"

"When, Blessed Virgin Mary? When?" Father Itcea addressed the Blessed Mother directly this time, convinced she spoke through Blanca, as she had through Bernadette at Lourdes.

"All this will come to pass, at the appointed hour." Blanca's voice grew quieter and quieter. "The people are not yet ready to receive this knowledge."

"What must we do to get ready?" asked Father Itcea.

The color had returned to Blanca's cheeks, and then her eyes blinked. "A new chapel . . ." Blanca seemed to say, her voice now barely a whisper. She stopped midsentence and sat up.

At that moment, Father Itcea heard a scrape on the wooden floor of the balcony.

I make my way down. I saw the girl collapse, but Father Itcea reached her before I could even shake off the shock. He impresses me with how compassionately he attends to her. Though I cannot understand her words, I can tell from the priest's expression that she has said something remarkable.

The tableau below hypnotizes me. like Jesus raising Tabitha from the dead, the priest kneels beside the girl, holding her hand as she rises to her feet.

"Is there anything I can do to help?" I ask.

The priest cranes his neck toward me. "William, I'm so glad you're here!" His voice is buoyant. "It's good I'm not the only witness to this astonishing event!"

The girl's dark brown eyes shine as if she has awakened from a beautiful dream.

"She seems fine now," he says. "Aren't you, Blanca?"

"Blanca"—what an apt name for her. The girl's skin glows as white as a lily. She says something in a thin, high-pitched voice.

"She's more than fine." Father Itcea sits Blanca down. "The Blessed Mother chose her to give us a message. Isn't it wonderful?"

He looks up at me expectantly.

"Unfortunately," I say, "I didn't understand what she said."

Father Itcea frowns.

"Perhaps you can tell me what she said, and I can write it down for you?"

A long pause transpires before he speaks. "That's a good idea, William. You can tell me what you saw, I can tell you what I heard, and we can write a statement together."

"Good idea," I answer.

Thunder claps over the dome.

"I want to take Blanca home first," he says. "I'll take her in my motorcar so that we don't get caught in the rain. I should be back by two o'clock, if you can come to the rectory then?"

I signal my assent. That gives me several hours to refresh my memory about supposed Marian apparitions so that I can participate knowledgeably in our conversation.

And I know exactly where to start. Years ago, I met a woman convinced she'd been cured by holy water at Lourdes. She painstakingly documented her experience in the hope that her evidence could one day be used to authenticate the apparitions of the Virgin Mary to Bernadette of Soubirous.

And I'd detailed her testimony in my journals.

Rain pelted the kitchen shutters at Blanca's family's farmhouse, creating a loud, thrumming noise. Father Itcea welcomed its interruption of the awkward silence. He had intended to speak to Blanca's father about her vision, but Joxemari wasn't home. Blanca sat warming herself and her doll by the hearth, staring into the fire.

Lightning flashed through the cracks in the shutters, and Blanca's mother, Maider, finally spoke. "The Blessed Mother has appeared to Blanca?" Her eyes flashed. "My daughter?"

"Difficult to believe, I know." Father Itcea noted a glossy image of a Madonna and Child, a page clipped from a magazine, taped to the wall over the mantel. "Yet the Virgin Mary has appeared to humble girls like her before. In France, for example, in La Salette-Fallavaux and in Paris." He could say more about these apparitions, among others, given his extensive training in Mariology. Instead, he touched the chain around his neck. "I always wear this Miraculous Medallion, as a reminder of my devotion to Mary."

Maider pulled her own necklace from beneath her blouse: on the medal, the Virgin Mary stood on a globe, crushing a serpent beneath her feet, rays shooting from her hands.

"I found this in my mother's jewelry box after she died," Maider said. "I remember Ama telling me about it when I was a little girl. Catherine Laboure woke up to a child's voice in the chapel and saw the Blessed Mother there. The Virgin Mary told Catherine, 'God wishes to charge you with a mission. You will be contradicted, but do not fear; you will have the grace to do what is necessary.'"

"Precisely." The priest tucked his medal back into his shirt and looked away. She seemed to know as much about this apparition as he did.

Maider stared intently at him.

He cleared his throat. "She also said that all who wear this medal will have graces bestowed on them. Perhaps Blanca is this grace for both of us: you as her mother and me as the priest who witnessed the Virgin Mary's first appearance to Blanca."

Joxemari walked in. "This was not the first time." He took off his beret and leaned on his cane. "I was there when she came to Blanca on Aranzibia Hill months ago."

The priest's mouth fell open and he looked at Blanca.

Blanca's cheeks flamed red.

Blanca's stomach churned. Why would Aita tell the priest about her visions? She hugged Rosa tightly, unable to speak.

"What is this?" Ama turned to Blanca, her tone sharp. "Have you been seeing things?"

Father Itcea glared at Blanca, then at Aita. "If the girl has seen the Virgin Mary before, I should have been told immediately." His jaw tightened. "Only men of the cloth have the authority to determine the veracity of such claims!"

Blanca teared up and bowed her head.

"Someone should at least have told *me*!" Ama frowned at Aita. "I am her mother!"

Her father sighed, then sat down. Blanca realized he'd probably been waiting for the priest's invitation to do so. He could no longer stand without pain.

Aita turned to Blanca. "I'm sorry about telling your secret without asking you first. I've already heard rumors about a girl from Indartze having visions. It was only a matter of time before they figured out who it was." He glanced at Father Itcea. "Now that the priest himself has witnessed your vision, there's no point in denying it."

He held Blanca's gaze and touched her hand, but that did not stop her tears. He had just given Refugio a woodworking lesson. Had Refugio told Aita that he knew about her visions? Had Refugio told other people?

She wiped her cheeks, then felt the comforting warmth of the Blessed Mother. Her soft brown eyes, Her long flaxen hair, Her soft voice and warm smile.

"I was too afraid to tell anyone," Blanca said.

She stared at the floor, bracing for more questions

"Nothing will happen to you if you tell the truth," Father Itcea said. "As you know from Mass today, God forgives all who confess their sins and promise to sin no more." He had softened his tone. "It's even better to avoid sins, of course, like lying about seeing the Virgin Mary before today."

"I would never lie about my Blessed Mother!" Blanca scrambled to her feet, letting Rosa fall to the earthen floor. "She is wise and kind and good! She chose me to *gaizkatu herria*—and I will do it!" Blanca felt the Blessed Mother's spirit move through her, and she remembered something else.

"She told me to do what's right and true," Blanca said. "To be ready to sacrifice!"

Blanca picked up her doll from the ground and held it over her head. "Sacrifice like this!" Then she threw Rosa into the fire.

CHAPTER SIXTEEN

Blanca ran to her room, threw herself on the bed, and burst into tears. She couldn't believe what she'd just done.

Thunder clapped above.

Blanca bolted upright. She looked around for something to hold onto, but it couldn't be a something childish like a doll.

"Meow!" Xuriko crept in through the bedroom window and jumped on the bureau. The cat stood beside a pointy object and groomed herself.

"What have you got there?" Blanca rose to pick up the keepsake from her grandmother's house. A small sharp-pointed crystal pyramid, which fit in Blanca's hand. Inside the pyramid stood a statue of Bernadette Soubirous kneeling before the Blessed Mother, a bed of roses at her feet.

The roses were red like the dress Aita had painted on her dolly, and Blanca fought back tears. "I'm sorry I had to sacrifice you, Rosa."

Xuriko jumped to sit on Blanca's lap, purred loudly, and looked up at Blanca with forgiving eyes.

Blanca pet her cat as she looked more closely at the knickknack. Over the Blessed Mother's head floated a halo composed of words.

The cat rubbed her nose against the pointed top. "*Kaxuman.* Be careful." Blanca took the souvenir away, worried the sharp edges would hurt Xuriko.

Blanca turned the object over and noticed the dates, from February to July 1858, engraved at the base.

"Eighteen dates," Blanca told Xuriko. "I think that's how many times the Blessed Mother appeared to Bernadette."

Xuriko purred more loudly.

Bernadette had received messages almost daily. Perhaps Blanca could *gaizkatu* sooner if she went up Aranzibia Hill more often?

The bells of Our Lady of Sorrows struck one.

If she left now, she would be able to make it to Aranzibia Hill and back before dark.

"I must take my leave now," said Father Itcea from the hallway. "I have an appointment, then I will begin hearing confessions at four o'clock."

That's right! Ama and Aita would be sure to go. But Father Itcea's instructions applied only to people over the age of discernment, thirteen for girls. In the barn below the house the cows bellowed as they did whenever Cruz came to milk them. Her parents would have no problem leaving her at home with her brother.

The priest's footsteps on the stairs pounding in her ears, Blanca clipped a coat around her neck in case it was cold on Aranzibia Hill. She took one more look at the Lourdes souvenir for courage and noted the rosary wrapped around Bernadette Soubirous's hands as she prayed. Amatxi Angeline had had lots of rosaries. Blanca sifted through the drawer where her mother had put them: rosaries made of blue enamel, mother-of-pearl, white silver, olive wood, and oak. But Blanca immediately knew which one she would take with her: the one with ruby red beads, exactly the color of Rosa's dress.

I sit in Father Itcea's office, taking my pen and notepad from my shirt pocket.

"It appears Blanca has been experiencing visions for months," he says. "She first saw the Virgin Mary in November of last year."

"Six months ago?" I say. "How did we not hear of it before now?" When villagers in Knock, Ireland, claimed to see the Virgin Mary, it took only a matter of days before pilgrims inundated the site and ruined it by chipping away at the gables to take home as souvenirs.

"Her father told her to tell no one, as Bernadette's parents initially forbade her," Father Itcea says. "Even so, Bernadette could not be dissuaded. Tens of thousands of pilgrims came to observe her receive the Virgin Mother's messages." His eyes gleam. "One of many similarities between the visions at Lourdes and ours!"

Ours? I jot the word down as a reminder of another similarity between this and other alleged apparitions: the rapidity with which clergy take credit for them and interpret them for their own ends.

"Such as . . . ?" I say.

"For instance, the Virgin Mary appeared to both girls in the mountains as they carried out their chores, demonstrating their dedication to duty and family, one might say." He speaks more quickly. "Bernadette was gathering firewood with her sister when the Virgin Mary came to her in the cave. Blanca was collecting mushrooms with her father when she appeared to her on Aranzibia Hill."

"I see." I have not yet been to Aranzibia Hill, though I've heard of it. "If memory serves," I say, "the Virgin Mary supposedly appeared to Bernadette of Soubirous multiple times." Historically speaking, Marian apparitions always indicate underlying political or social tumult. In this case, probably the recent elections and exile of the king. Yet I need to capture the locals' point of view for my story, and the best way to do that is to keep the priest talking.

"Fifteen days in succession," he says. "Then there are the similarities in the messages she gave to Bernadette and Blanca. At Lourdes the Virgin Mary called herself the Immaculate Conception, affirming that she alone was born without Original Sin. This reinforced the pope's authority over the rationalists. On Aranzibia Hill, the Virgin Mary enjoined Blanca to *gaizkatu herria*, or liberate the country." Father Itcea's voice rose in pitch. "Clearly, this calls us to purify Spain of the nonbelievers now running this country. When the Virgin Mary spoke to Blanca today—rather, to me, through Blanca—she said something about rebuilding the church as well. Though Blanca regained consciousness before she could convey the entire message."

"She did seem . . . disoriented," I say.

"As evidenced by that otherworldly voice Blanca used when speaking for the Blessed Mother," he says. "You must have noticed that, even if you didn't understand what she said."

"Now that you mention it, I see what you mean." I write down what I really think: children are natural mimics and love attention. This girl can easily put on that voice and pretend to be speaking as the Virgin Mary.

"And, of course, the scent of roses permeated the area when Blanca was in vision," Father Itcea adds. "It filled my nostrils. It's one of the ways to confirm a vision as genuine."

"Because roses have long been a symbol of the Virgin Mary," I say, though I did not catch a whiff of roses.

"Then, Bernadette of Soubirous and Blanca look remarkably similar," he says. "Blanca comes from a poor peasant family, so she is not as well nourished as she could be. Thus, like Bernadette, she is small for her age and prone to illness. Her parents told me today that she has suffered fainting spells and convulsions."

"Uh-huh," I say, afraid to look at the priest directly lest I reveal my disdain. If Blanca is so malnourished and sickly, why doesn't the Church draw on its considerable riches to help her?

The priest fishes two photographs from his desk drawer, one of Bernadette of Soubirous and another of Blanca. "Doesn't Blanca look just like Bernadette?"

"They both do have fair skin, dark eyes and hair." *As most girls in these parts do.* I pick up the photos. "Is there something else in their look that you find significant?"

I turn the photos over as I do with artifacts to check provenance. If the priest is answering my question, I don't hear him. For on the back of the one photo, I read, "Blanca Gurrutxetegia, daughter of Maider of Bayonne."

Maider—"beloved"—whom I call Caireann, the name in Irish.

Blanca is my beloved's daughter.

I let go of the photos but hold tightly to my pen, forcing it to move across the pad as Father Itcea talks, glad my long habit of writing in Irish with the letters close together will not betray that I write gibberish.

Is my long-lost love here? Why haven't I seen her?

"William?" Father Itcea's voice seems far away. "William? Are you all right? Your hands are shaking."

"*No se preocupe*—don't worry about me." I feel my face warm. "I probably just need a cigarette."

"By all means." Father Itcea opens the shutter and window behind him.

"Never mind." I pat my shirt pocket with the Gauloises and try to smile. "Perhaps I'll work with more focus if I have a smoke to look forward to when I'm done."

"Yes." Father Itcea returns a smile. "Why don't you tell me what you observed of Blanca in vision and I can write it down? Per our initial plan?"

"Good idea," I reply. But now that I know Blanca is Caireann's daughter, how can I provide an objective account of what I saw?

"It seems we are in agreement about the basic parameters of the vision." The priest takes out a fresh sheet of paper. "That there are striking similarities between the Virgin Mother's appearances to Bernadette at Lourdes and what we witnessed today with Blanca, which strongly suggest that the girl's vision is real."

I find myself nodding even though my understanding does not accord with his. "Of course, some might argue that the commonalities between the two cases are pure coincidence," I say. "Skeptics, I mean." Until I learned that Blanca is Caireann's daughter, like them I might have questioned the visions. The Caireann I courted was guileless, a devout Catholic; she would never raise a daughter who could fabricate a visitation by the Virgin Mary.

"Yes, we must make an argument based on reason as much as on faith," the priest says. "We Jesuits have always held that the two go hand in hand."

Though surprised to learn this, it gives me an idea. "A disbeliever might reason, for example, that Blanca only thought she saw the Virgin Mary. That her vision is a symptom of insanity."

"I've anticipated that," Father Itcea says. "The same argument was made with other seers. With Bernadette, rigorous medical investigations by the most respected doctors proved she was of sound mind."

I tremble to think what this rigor entailed.

"In fact, Bernadette became renown for her lucidity in conveying the Virgin Mary's messages and for the single-minded pursuit of the Blessed Mother's purpose." Father Itcea's pupils widen. "Fulfilling the Virgin Mary's request for penance, Bernadette freely accepted the unremitting pain that came her way, dying in agony at age thirty-five."

Shivers go up my spine at the prospect of such a little girl as Blanca enduring such suffering.

"For the apparitions at Knock," I say, "the investigating commission also considered whether the apparitions emanated from natural causes." I flip through my notes. "You mentioned that Blanca first saw the Virgin Mary while collecting mushrooms. A doubter might argue that her vision was only a hallucination brought on by the poisonous varieties."

"Even a city boy like me would never make that mistake," Father Itcea says. "All Basques can tell the good mushrooms from the bad. Even if this were not the case, how would one explain Blanca's vision inside the church this morning?"

"Hmmm," I say. "Do you know Blanca's whereabouts before Mass? Perhaps she had to cross a field from her home to get to Our Lady of Sorrows?"

The priest furrows his brow. "Her family's farmhouse is quite high up in the hills. Her mother told me her son walked Blanca to Mass." He writes something on his piece of paper. "I shall inquire as to the exact route next time I see them."

Ah, that would explain why I have not seen Caireann: she does not live in Indartze proper but in a remote farmhouse. And judging from Father Itcea's previous comments, one that struggles to provide for the family. I am devastated at the downturn in Caireann's circumstances. We had dreamed of building such a wonderful life together.

"This is helpful, William. You're playing devil's advocate," says Father Itcea, a sparkle in his eyes. "I've made a list of other objections cynics might make of

Blanca's apparitions. For instance, some might quibble that Aranzibia Hill is an inauspicious site for Mary to appear, given its history of . . ."

I cannot focus on his words. Something about witches having lived there hundreds of years ago, and how the Virgin Mary often appears to common people in nature. Ordinarily I would relish these details and take copious notes. But all I can think of is that Caireann's daughter is about to ignite a religious frenzy. And history has not been kind to little girls who purport to have visions of the divine.

CHAPTER SEVENTEEN

Touching the beads of her grandmother's red rosary, Blanca marched up Aranzibia Hill. The dark clouds over her family's farmhouse had given way to clearer skies, and Blanca sweat under her coat. She shook away the memory of the first time she'd come up here with only her doll for company. Rosa had given her such courage.

"I'll say a Rosary for you, Rosa." Blanca took a bead to her lips. That's what they'd done for Amatxi Angeline, right before the funeral. Before she could begin praying the first decade, she heard a male voice singing.

Agur, Maria, graziaz betea	Hail Mary, full of grace
Jauna da zurekin	The Lord is with you

Its otherworldly tone captivated her.

Benedikatua zare	Blessed are you
Emazte guzien artean	Among all women

Blanca hiked toward the voice. "Refugio!" she said. "What are you doing up here?"

Refugio blushed. "I sing to the Blessed Mother whenever I finish part of her chapel."

In the middle of the grove, in front of the cross Refugio had already erected, an altar now stood.

"When did you have time to do all this?" Blanca touched the altar. The wood was sanded smooth and into it was fitted the rectangular plaque dedicated to the woman Sabine.

"I come up here whenever I can," Refugio answered. "I thought this afternoon was a good time, as all the grown-ups should be at confession."

Smart boy, Blanca thought. She also wondered if Refugio avoided going to Our Lady of Sorrows altogether. Aita had told her that many people still didn't want *agotas* going to "their" church.

"I like what you did with the plaque," Blanca said.

"I decided the plate itself wasn't long enough for the altar, so I made it the centerpiece instead." Refugio ran his fingers over the letters of the inscription. They were now neatly scrubbed and glistened in the sunlight. "What do you think?"

"It's beautiful!" Blanca stood beside Refugio, one hand on her rosary and the other lingering over the inscription's last line: *"Bizi berria—*A new life."

A tingling sensation traveled from her fingertips, up her arms, to her heart, and down her legs to her feet. Her cheeks warmed and she felt dizzy.

"Blanca," Refugio asked, "do you feel faint?" He tried to seat her on a tree stump nearby, but Blanca lay down on the ground instead. She stretched her arms out straight.

Refugio seemed to be saying something to her, fear in his voice, though he sounded far away.

The voice of the Blessed Mother whispered through the trees, crystal clear.

"Blanca, my child," she said, "I am pleased you have come today. I have a special message for you to give to the people."

"Yes, Ama Maite Maria!" Blanca couldn't move, but the image at the treetops gave her solace: the Blessed Mother wore a simple white blouse and flowing skirt, a halo around her blue veil. Over her head floated a dove, its wings unfolding.

The Blessed Mother looked at Blanca with her soft brown eyes. "You must tell the people a time of terrible trial is coming." Her tone remained calm despite the danger revealed in her words. "The faithful will suffer severely, and many will be lost."

Blanca's whole body twitched. Would these trials affect her own family? Would they be among those lost?

"Do not worry," the Blessed Mother assured her. "In the end, with your help, the righteous will triumph."

The burden of the message weighed on Blanca. How would she even know who or what was righteous? She tried to ask the Blessed Mother but choked on the words.

Then everything went black.

A Gaulois at my lips, I look over my notes from my conversation with Father Itcea. They are even messier than usual. I'll have to go back to my lodgings early to decipher them. I glance at Old Simon, his expression as impenetrable as always. He wipes down the bar and chitchats with his customers. I try to catch his attention to order a drink, when a young man rushes in, panting for breath. Perspiration drips from his heavy brow and soaks through his shirt.

He says something in Basque, agony in his voice. The bar falls silent and the customers clear a path as Sofia makes her way toward the boy. Old Simon sits him on a barstool and brings him a glass of water.

As the three huddle together, I realize who the young man is: the *agota* boy the mob kicked out of the dance. He speaks in spurts and starts.

"Comrades," Sofia says in Castilian, "a young girl has collapsed on Aranzibia Hill."

Murmurs of shock and concern arise.

"*Oi Ama!*" A woman's voice calls out. "My goodness!"

"What was she doing up that witches' mountain?" a male voice asks.

"Who is it?" a second woman asks.

Sofia raises her hand and hushes the crowd. "Blanca Gurrutxetegia," she answers.

Caireann's daughter! I tuck my notebook away.

"She is breathing but not moving," Sofia says. "She is not bleeding and doesn't appear to have any injuries, but Refugio couldn't wake her up. We need to get her down right away."

My mind races: What can I do without being seen as the meddling foreigner? With my long legs and years of experience traversing difficult terrain, I can make it up the mountain more quickly than most people here.

Sofia signals her sentries, who immediately recruit other muscular young men. They make their way toward Sofia and Refugio. The other patrons fall back.

"You four." Sofia names each man in turn. "Take Refugio to Blanca. Carry him if you have to."

"That won't be necessary." Refugio stands up. "I can make it on my own."

A stout middle-aged woman approaches Sofia, and they speak among themselves in Basque. They remind me of the conclaves of women I've seen throughout my travels whenever a problem in the community needed solving.

I tap the Basque man beside me, hoping he speaks Castilian. "*Quién es?*" I ask. "Who is she?"

"*La curandera* Remedios," he whispers reverently. "The healer."

"Shouldn't we call a doctor?" I say.

Sofia looks at me, fire in her eyes. "There are no doctors in these parts."

Remedios exits the bar with the men and Refugio. The remaining patrons look at Sofia expectantly. I leave money on the bar and move closer to the door. I will go with the rescue team whether invited or not.

"I will notify the family," Sofia says.

Women exchange knowing looks.

"*Buena idea*—good idea," a woman says, nodding.

"They will be so worried," says another.

"What can we do to help?" Several people voice the question. They could do any number of things to assist poor Blanca and her family: prepare food for them or take on their chores, freeing them to focus on the girl's care.

So I am shocked at Sofia's answer.

"Pray." She turns and exits the bar.

Father Itcea hung his vestments in the sacristy closet and heard the rumblings in his stomach the litany of confessions had drowned out. He'd thought it impossible to exaggerate the depths of guilt abiding in the Basque soul. He'd been wrong: his parishioners had enthusiastically embraced the opportunity to partake in the Sacrament of Penance. They'd detailed all manner of sin: untruths told, indiscretions committed, jealousies harbored. Some had confessed serious sins (desecrating the sanctity of marriage, the primary failing) and expressed obvious relief at absolution. No one had admitted to taking the sacred objects from Our Lady of Sorrows. Yet.

Still, the residue of his flock's moral detritus stuck to him. He craved a drink to wash it all away. He approached Bar Herria, his mouth watering at the thought of the appetizers he would likely find there.

Instead, a barrage of words came at him.

Diós te salve, Maria	God saves you, Mary
Llena eres de gracia	Full of grace
El Señor es contigo	The Lord is with you

Father Itcea's jaw dropped. Everyone in the bar, including Old Simon, was praying the Rosary on their knees! Finding no room on the floor, the priest sat on a barstool, stifling a groan that he would have to wait longer for his drink.

Bendita tú eres	Blessed are you
Entre todas las mujeres	Among all women

Y bendito es el fruto	And blessed is the fruit
De tu vientre, Jesús	Of your womb, Jesus

As he prayed, Father Itcea thought, *My confessions had more power than I thought!* He'd clearly inspired his parishioners to continue their penance here.

Santa Maria, Madre de Dios	Hail Mary, Mother of God
Ruega por nosotros, pecadores	Pray for us sinners

Before Mass, Doña Carmen would lead the congregation in the Rosary. A woman he didn't know presided over this group.

Ahora y en la hora	Now and in the hour
De nuestra muerte	Of our death
Amen	Amen

Father Itcea considered taking over her role but decided it wasn't worth the trouble. Perfunctorily joining the gathering in the Lord's Prayer that concluded the Rosary decade, he looked at the bowed heads but didn't recognize most of these people. He peeked at Old Simon; the tavern owner's face betrayed only pain. Old Simon had suffered a leg injury in the war in Cuba, the priest remembered. It must be agony for him to kneel this long on the wooden floor.

Finally, the prayers concluded and Father Itcea could find out what was going on.

"*Oración de Lourdes,*" the woman intoned, touching a bead on her rosary. "Prayer to Our Lady of Lourdes."

Oh, no. Father Itcea would not sit through another decade.

"My dear parishioners," he began as he stood up, "I am pleased you have chosen to continue your contrition in such an . . . unusual venue."

The woman leading the prayers kept her fingers on a bead, much as a seamstress holding her place by embedding her needle in fabric.

"I assure you: your confessions at Our Lady of Sorrows have expiated your sins." Father Itcea waited to see relief wash over the people's faces.

They stared blankly at him.

They probably don't understand what "expiated" means.

Father Itcea looked more closely at the crowd as he searched for a synonym. These weren't the people who came to confession today. So what had inspired such fervent pleas to the Virgin Mary?

The woman leader seemed to read his mind. "We do not pray to beg the Virgin Mary for forgiveness," she said.

The priest did not appreciate her contemptuous tone.

"We pray that she might keep the girl Blanca safe. The girl collapsed on Aranzibia Hill."

"Blanca has collapsed?" Alarm shot through Father Itcea. "Take me to her immediately!"

CHAPTER EIGHTEEN

I follow the lights of the rescue party at a respectful distance. It will be dark soon, so I am glad they'd had the forethought to bring torches with them. My ignorance of the Basque language has deprived me of my usual ability to build rapport with the local community. I do not recall seeing any of these people, except for Refugio, at Bar Herria before today.

"*Más rápido,*" the *curandera* says. "Go faster."

"*Sí, vamos!* Let's go!" says the taller of Sofia's sentries.

Both of them speak Castilian!

They march silently except for the occasional encouragements from one to the other.

"*Perdóname*—excuse me." I catch up to the bodyguard. "I heard about the girl who fell and would like to offer my assistance."

The group slows its pace to glance at me; only Sofia's sentry takes a long look.

"I helped carry wounded soldiers off battlefields in the Great War," I say.

"I recognize you," he says. Then he addresses the crowd: "He's a friend of Old Simon's."

The group continues its march. The bodyguard holds out his hand to me. "My name is Michel."

"I have a brother named Michael," I say. I wonder if this young man is also named after the archangel from Revelations, the leader of God's army against evil. "I am called William. Guillermo, if you prefer."

"*Mucho gusto*—pleased to meet you," Michel says. "Any friend of Old Simon's is a friend of mine. He lets us use his bar for our meetings."

I nod. Old Simon's life is more complicated than he lets on. He must know the assembly's politics collide with his wife's beliefs.

"This is my first time up Aranzibia." I hope I pronounce the name correctly. "How long will it take to reach the top?"

Michel shakes his head. "I've never been there."

Ah—that's why Sofia has sent Refugio with the search party despite his obvious exhaustion.

"Refugio," Michel calls out, "how much longer?"

"Any minute now," Remedios answers instead. "We're taking a secret shortcut."

That usually means a long-abandoned trail that could easily get people lost. Wouldn't it be better to use the more certain route Refugio knows, as Sofia has directed?

The *curandera* lets me catch up. "Do not worry," she whispers. "We healers have been visiting the summit for hundreds of years. We call it Sabine's shrine, after the wise woman who once lived there."

The name rings a bell, but I'm too worried about Blanca to make further inquiries.

We reach the top and there lies little Blanca on her back, her face contorted in pain. I try to go to her but my feet feel as heavy as lead. I regard the others; they too stand rigid, an odd mix of awe and terror on their faces.

Her round eyes moist with tears, Blanca shouts at the treetops.

"The Chastisement will soon be upon us!" she says with urgency. "Our Blessed Mother says there will come a darkness!"

Blanca squirms as though trying to disentangle herself from invisible ties that bind her. She screams and shakes her head. I stand mesmerized, my heart in my throat, still unable to move. The rest of the rescue party also remain transfixed.

"The darkness will last three days!" Blanca's voice is deep and hoarse again.

"Our Lady speaks through her," the *curandera* says. "We must listen!" She falls to her knees and everybody follows suit. Even I cannot resist her command.

"After the darkness, a terrifying hurricane will blow from the northwest!" Blanca says. "Great gusts of wind will collide and bring a storm that will lift people into the air!"

Hurricanes rarely if ever hit the Atlantic Peninsula. This prediction cannot be correct. Flurries blow through the grove as if to admonish me.

"It's coming! Please save us!" pleads one of the men.

"Santa Maria!" a woman calls out. "Pray for us!"

Others in the crowd make their own pleas.

"Have no fear!" Remedios assures them. "This is a holy place! Our Lady speaks to this girl!"

We fall silent, waiting for Blanca to speak again. My hands shake. Though a cigarette would calm my nerves, I don't dare light up.

"The hurricane will ravage the earth!" Blanca says. "People will flee from their homes, go from place to place, lost!"

Like me, everyone in the rescue party remains kneeling. Their lips move in silent prayer while mine do not. The healer and Refugio have moved closer to Blanca, forming a triptych: the healer kneels at Blanca's right side and holds that hand in hers; Refugio mirrors the healer's position on the left side.

"The power of my Son Jesus, with the sword of the archangel Michael, will smite the evildoers!" Blanca says. "The earth will open up and bury the persecutors!"

"Blessed Mother, pray for us!" Michel calls out.

"Millions will fall, crushed like snowflakes into a burning hole!" Blanca's gaze softens and her body ceases its twitching. "Afterward, the world will be at peace," she says more softly, "and the people content and blessed, because faithfulness will reign. What will become of those who mock and persecute the faith?"

I sense movement behind me and steel myself for a torrent of pleas and prayers. Terror fills Refugio's eyes, and the other young men look ready to bolt down the mountain.

Only the *curandera* remains calm. She feels Blanca's forehead, then her wrist. "She's coming out of her trance."

A breeze wafts through the treetops. A smile spreads across Blanca's face, and her cheeks slowly return to a rosy hue. She sits up and looks around quizzically, settling on Refugio.

"What happened?" she asks, her voice childlike again. "What are you all doing up here?"

Before Refugio can answer comes the thud of heavy footsteps, Father Itcea's.

"That's what I would like to know!" the priest demands.

Panting for breath, Father Itcea looked around. In the middle of the grove stood the foundations of a chapel! The rising full moon illuminated a beechwood cross twice as high as he was tall. On top of this lay a wreath of red roses, whose intense scent infused the cold air. A waist-high rectangular table stood before the cross.

Clearly that was intended to be an altar. And instead of a sanctioned man of the cloth, Blanca presided there. Her black coat, fastened at the neck like a chasuble, emphasized the white linen of her blouse. A blood red rosary wound around her right wrist like the stigmata. A dozen people gathered around her with bated breath, like the apostles awaiting Christ's wisdom at the Last Supper.

"Are you having Mass up here without me?" Father Itcea clenched his jaw.

The priest looked around at the silent gathering. Mostly young men and a middle-aged woman he'd seen about town. He knew the names of only three people: Blanca, Refugio—and William.

How did that foreigner get wind of this before me?

He readied himself to confront William, to demand to know what he and these others were doing up here. Then he decided that doing so would elevate William's status. No, better to ignore him.

Father Itcea instead turned his attention to Blanca. "My child," he asked, in the even tone he used for the Sacrament of Penance, "what is it you are doing up here?" He let his question linger—a strategy that worked well in extracting confessions.

A northern wind swirled from the treetops to the altar. The torchlights flickered on Blanca's face, shining with a wide smile. She inclined her head and fixed her gaze on a point high up.

"Yes, Ama Maite Maria," she said. "I will tell them."

A brief pause, and the girl turned to Father Itcea.

"The Most Blessed Mother has told me that this year will bring great political and social revolutions," she said. "There will be wars and upheaval."

The juxtaposition of Blanca's stark message with her thin, high-pitched voice jarred Father Itcea. He glanced at William; this was not the low, gravelly voice Blanca had used during her vision in Our Lady of Sorrows.

William stared at Blanca, his fingers twitching.

"On the day of the Great Miracle, beginning at five in the afternoon," Blanca said, "the Blessed Mother will appear on Aranzibia Hill with a half-moon at her feet that will give off light in all four directions." The girl's face lit up.

Father Itcea beamed. This was a clear reference to the Book of Revelations! Where everyone will finally see the truth for themselves!

"*Mirakuilua!*" a woman said breathlessly. "A miracle!"

His cheeks wet with tears, the *agota* boy held onto Blanca as if she were a porcelain doll.

"On the day of the miracle, some will see the Blessed Mother, others only her shadow." Blanca blinked intermittently. "Some will see nothing at all."

Her gaze rested on William at those words, Father Itcea noticed.

The color drained from her face and she sobbed. "The Blessed Mother says that the Chastisement will come before the Great Miracle!" Her voice trembled and rose in pitch.

Refugio struggled to keep her in his arms. The *curandera* took Blanca's hands in hers.

"There will be a rain of fire and a cloud of snakes and sudden deaths! The wicked will perish!" Blanca said through tears. "The more one walks, the more dead one will find!"

Father Itcea's pulse raced at this prediction.

"Between the Chastisement and the Great Miracle, there will be little time," Blanca wailed, rocking back and forth in Refugio's arms. She gripped the hands of the woman, who grimaced in pain.

Her pain would pale in comparison with the punishment his parishioners would suffer in hell if they did not repent of their sins before the miracle.

"The Blessed Mother has told me on which day the Chastisement will come!"

"*Cuándo? Noiz?* When?" The question burst from the lips of all those gathered, even William.

Then Blanca screamed and fell back into Refugio's arms. Her face blanched and her lips turned blue.

Father Itcea rushed toward Blanca, holding a hand up in warning. "Let's give her room!" The priest had ministered to the ill many times.

"With respect, Father," the woman said. "I have seen such trances before and know what to do."

Taken aback at her audacity, the priest did not respond. The other men, except for Refugio and William, whispered urgently among themselves.

The woman laid Blanca gently onto the ground. Only the trickling of water could be heard.

"You hear that?" the woman said. "That's Sabine's spring. It's been curing people for hundreds of years. And it'll help Blanca now."

Blanca lay exhausted, her gaze fixed on a halo of light growing bigger and bigger. She could see the broad trunks and tops of trees but nothing else within the encircling brightness. Then the radiance enveloped her as well, casting everything outside it into shadow. Her fingers and toes tingled and her head spun. She let the brilliance in.

"Blessed Mother," she asked, "are you still there?"

"I am here, my child," replied a voice from the light.

Blanca focused on the luminous sight: dressed in a flowing white gown, the Blessed Mother wore no crown or veil over her long golden hair. A royal blue shawl draped her left shoulder. She clasped her hands together over her heart.

Surrounded by cherubs circling overhead, the Blessed Mother inclined her head upward.

"Ama Maite Maria!" exclaimed Blanca. "How I long to be among your angels!"

The Blessed Mother's loving expression made her weep.

"I am always with you." The Blessed Mother gestured to her in invitation, and Blanca reached out, feeling herself floating up to her through the sky. She longed to be enfolded in her embrace. Blanca's heart filled with joy to become one with the Blessed Mother's, whose heart Blanca could now see on her bodice. Little roses encircled the Blessed Mother's red heart, which pulsated rays of light.

"This is my Sacred Heart," the Blessed Mother said. "It throbs with the pain of my people. They will come here seeking sanctuary from their suffering. You must help them when they come."

The Blessed Mother took Blanca's hand and placed it on her own heart. Blanca thrilled that their two hearts beat in time.

"Yes, Ama!" Blanca blurted out the words while tears of joy trickled down her cheeks. So long as the Blessed Mother was with her, Blanca could handle any pain, her own or someone else's.

Blanca wanted to say so much: how honored she felt be to chosen as the Blessed Mother's messenger and instrument for healing, how she would try her best to be worthy of being chosen. She took deep breaths, straining for the right words to express herself.

Water moistened her cheeks even though she'd stopped crying. And the Blessed Mother faded away, her white dress blending into the full moon that now hung over the grove.

"She's coming out of the spell!" a female voice said

Blanca raised herself to a seated position and shook her head to clear her vision. A portly middle-aged woman was kneeling beside her, holding a vial of clear liquid. By the light of the flashlights and that of the moon, Blanca could see a handful of other people standing or crouching around her: Refugio, Father Itcea, and that tall man with the messy ginger hair she'd seen at Our Lady of Sorrows.

"She's all right," the priest called out, and the others exhaled with relief. The red-headed man seemed the most reassured.

"When will the Chastisement come?" a male voice cried out.

Blanca didn't know what he was talking about.

"Thanks be to God!" Father Itcea said. "Let us pray—."

Urgent footsteps stamped through the brush.

"—Let's not!"

It was Cruz, his shirt wet with perspiration.

Cruz points a finger at the priest, his other hand on his hip. A righteous anger emanates from him, an anger I recognize from my own youth. He whispers to Blanca, then consults quietly with the *curandera*. He takes a swig from his bota bag.

"We'll do what I say," Cruz says, his Castilian greatly improved. "I'm her family." He stares down the priest.

"My son." The priest moves toward Cruz, his hands up in supplication. "I know you want to help your sister. So do I." He approaches the area behind the altar where Blanca, Cruz, and the healer huddle. "An extraordinary event has transpired here today. Your sister has been chosen to receive messages from above . . ."

Cruz mutters something and gives Remedios a velvet pouch, the kind used to store valuable necklaces or earrings. Remedios intones some Basque words in singsong. The only word I recognized is "Maria." Then she takes a necklace out of the pouch and puts it around Blanca's neck. My flashlight shines on the pendant; made of garnet, it is in the form of the head of the Virgin Mary.

"This will keep Blanca safe," Cruz says. "It contains the relics of our ancestor Maria, burnt at the stake—"

All at once Blanca falls back. Her face turns toward me, grows waxy, and her eyes widen, staring. A frisson chills my back. I rush toward Blanca and see the priest doing the same.

Cruz and the healer gesture for us to stay back. We obey.

He touches Blanca's forehead and cheeks, tenderly, concern and fear clouding his eyes. "She is unconscious."

Remedios puts her hand on his and whispers something to him.

Cruz stands up, calm and steady now except for the twitching of his fingers. "We need to get Blanca home so Remedios can treat her."

He scans the group and exhales, as if unhappy with his options. He turns to Remedios.

She nods in my direction.

"*Señor.*" Cruz approaches me. "Will you help me carry my sister home?"

CHAPTER NINETEEN

Cruz and I follow the light of the torch Remedios holds up through the fog as we round the last bend to Caireann's farmhouse. We carry Blanca between us. Cruz walks backward, holding his sister beneath her arms; I grip Blanca under her knees. I'm grateful for the glow the full moon casts upon us. The rest of the rescue party have gone their separate ways, taking their flashlights with them.

Remedios has told me that the name of Caireann's farmhouse, *Gurrutxetegia*, means "place of the cross." How fitting. I left Caireann temporarily to pursue my professional ambitions, and she quickly replaced me with someone else. That is my cross to bear, and the hour-long descent gives me time to agonize over my decision. We have made the journey in almost complete silence. Remedios speaks only to direct us through the quickest path. The stoic Cruz limps when we traverse rocky terrain, as if nursing an injury. Every so often, I signal I want to pause so that he can rest without admitting weakness.

I look for a place to do so again as the outline of the farmhouse emerges through the fog. A breeze kicks up. The tinny sound of a swing swaying in the breeze draws my attention to a large oak tree to my right. Its huge roots buckle up from the ground like a fist; on these, plywood has been nailed to form a bench. I nod in that direction, and we settle Blanca there.

Cruz sits beside her, cooing a tune and brushing her hair away from her forehead. "She's breathing more easily," he says.

I nod. Some rosiness now touches Blanca's cheeks and she sighs as she nuzzles against her brother. But Cruz looks spent. He has taken off his left shoe and sock, his foot swollen and lacerated.

Remedios reaches the front door. "I'll let them know Blanca's here. I will need help in getting her upstairs."

"*Con permiso?* May I?" I ask Cruz, taking Blanca into my arms.

I approach Remedios, carrying Blanca.

Inside, my torment swells. *This is it. I will finally see Caireann again.* I have hoped for this moment for almost twenty years. In my fantasies we pick up where we left off—we weep, embrace, and resume our lives together as if nothing has changed. Deep down, though, I know this happy scenario is impossible.

The sound of Remedios knocking on the door brings me back to reality. Even in the moonlight, I can see the disrepair of the house. The whitewash has worn off the walls; chipped clay shingles dot the roof; the thistle over the lintel hangs dead. Caireann will open the door and see in me but a shell of the man she once loved. I'll surely compare unfavorably with the attractive and vigorous husband a woman as beautiful as Caireann would have found to love her.

I sweat in anticipation.

"I forgot," Remedios says. "We need the signal." She whistles twice, pauses, then whistles again. The piercing sound jostles more memories: how Caireann would sing those tear-jerking Basque songs as I accompanied her on the fiddle; the names we'd come up with for our future children—Basque ones for the boys, Irish for the girls. Or the look on her face when I last saw her, in 1913, when I told her I was returning to my native land to cover politics for *The Irish Times*, quite the coup for a budding journalist. I'd promised to return to Bayonne as soon as I made enough money to marry her. I didn't foresee the political tumult and violence the Home Rule movement would occasion, nor how the Great War would make civilian travel almost impossible.

What will it be like to see her again?

Footsteps plod down the stairs inside the house. The door swings open and a man old enough to be Caireann's father stands there: he's perhaps sixty-five years old, balding, stout, and supporting himself on a staff. He exchanges words with Remedios, then looks at me.

His jaw tightens and his eyes narrow.

"I am Blanca's father." He sets his cane aside and extends his arms to me. "I'll take her from here."

Not even a word of thanks?

"Joxemari," Remedios says, "don't you know what this man has done? If it weren't for him—"

"—I know what he's done," Joxemari replies. He gently places Blanca over one shoulder, like a shepherd with an injured lamb, and slams the door in my face.

Father Itcea had witnessed a miracle and wanted to broadcast the news as widely as possible. He hurried into the rectory, switched on the lights, loosened his Roman collar, and sat down at his desk. The grandfather clock chimed one o'clock in the morning; he didn't care.

From his studies of Mariology, he knew apparitions were more likely to be verified when viewed by masses of people. Except for Cruz and William, the other witnesses had listened rapt to Blanca's messages as they knelt before her. Not all had ascended Aranzibia Hill as believers. The young men wore the red-and-blue three-cornered hat, the emblem of the atheistic Communist party.

An owl hooted from the distance. Its call had echoed through the trees all the way down Aranzibia Hill. If the priest moved quickly, he could disseminate the news of Blanca's visions before the unbelievers had a chance to discredit them, and he could find a way to keep the girl safe from sycophants.

The moonlight cast its soft glow on the handball court. There, Father Itcea had first spoken to Cruz, soliciting his feedback on his homily commanding the men of his parish to vote for monarchist candidates. The priest recalled the spark he'd seen in the young man's eyes.

"Spain could use strong recruits like him," Father Itcea remembered thinking. He might be right about that, though Cruz would be fighting for the other side.

The owl hooted again, sounding closer this time. Father Itcea peeked out of the shutters, surprised to see a boy running across the handball court toward the rectory, carrying a bag.

"*Ave Maria*! What's this?" Father Itcea fastened his collar and walked toward the front door. He would not be caught looking undignified in his own home.

Two raps on the door, then the priest answered it.

The *agota* boy waited at the threshold.

"Aita Itcea." Refugio removed his cap. "Forgive me for bothering you at this hour. I have something important to tell you." He held tightly to the cloth bag.

Well I have something important to do. Father Itcea tamped down his growing irritation. "You will need to return later today—"

"—With respect, Father." Refugio blocked the door with his foot. "It cannot wait. It's about Blanca."

"What is it, my boy?" the priest asked. "Is she all right?"

"Blanca told me the Blessed Mother asked her to build a chapel on Aranzibia Hill." Refugio revealed a velvet bag inside the cloth one, and unwrapped some objects from it. "And Blanca asked me to help. Her father's been teaching me carpentry." He looked away, sheepishly. "But I came across . . . these items . . . and I placed them beneath the altar plaque. It was when Blanca touched the plaque that she fell into that trance."

Father Itcea stared at the items in Refugio's shaking hands: these were Father Zabaleta's valuable Eucharistic vessels! He should be incensed that this *agota* boy, whom he had saved from that mob, had stolen such sacred objects or had accepted them from the robbers.

Then a calm came over the priest. He remembered the glow emanating from that innocent girl as the Virgin Mary spoke through her. How peaceful and joyful he had felt as he watched Blanca in vision.

"Do come in, my boy." Father Itcea moved aside.

These sacred objects should be installed in the new chapel on Aranzibia Hill. Who knew what magnificent prophecies Blanca might foretell if displayed there with his blessing?

The bells of Our Lady of Sorrows tolled six, but Father Itcea had long been awake. Inspired by his long talk with Refugio and by the pile of newspapers sent by Gabriel that he'd finished reading last night, he had thought of the perfect way to bring attention to Blanca's visions: he would write verses for *Gure Txoko*. Though simple people like Refugio couldn't read, there was a long custom in the Basque Country of transmitting information by singing *bertsos*.

A robin trilling outside his window, Father Itcea had come up with three verses so far:

Maria, Aranzibian	Mother, on Aranzibia
Azaltzen zerana	You have appeared
Fededunok ara or	We, the faithful, go there
Baizaizu zuguna	To see you
Egunero, bostetan	Every day at five
Eskatu duzun bezala	As you asked
Mirakuilua	To see the miracle
Or gertatzen dana	Happening there

He wrote the lyrics to a traditional tune with a meter known to most Basques, famous for their ability to memorize songs, even after only one hearing. To make the story accessible to foreigners, the priest had also used the Castilian-inspired word for "miracle"—*mirakuilua*—in the hopes that it might pique the interests of the many outsiders who had begun to frequent Bar Herria.

Gaiztoak indar dute	The wicked are very powerful now
Zori txarrez orain	Unfortunately

Eta guzian jarri	And they are in charge
Zaizkigu buruz gain	Of all of us
Nun nai eginez dabiltz	They are everywhere
Nai duten aña irain	Doing whatever they want
Zure laguntzaz	With your help
Bagera debrua'n lain	We will best the devil

Debrua—"devil"—that should capture the reader's attention, given its similarity to the Castilian *diablo*. Father Itcea imagined the bar's patrons huddling together, anxious to hear what evil the devil had wrought this time.

Ez bada menderatzen	If we do not conquer
Debruaren indarra	The power of the wicked
Ondatzera dijoa	They will ruin
Gure herri zala	The Basque Country
Onerano ez dedin	May that not happen
Gaizokiko gara	We beg you
Eskatzen degu zure	We ask for your help
Laguntza goitara	From above

Herri, in the middle line, could be interpreted as "the people" or "the land." Who wouldn't want the Virgin Mary to protect those they loved?

The robin peeped again as the clock pinged the quarter hour. Father Itcea had to get ready for Mass soon, but another rush of words came to him.

Ama lagundu bada	May Mother Mary give help
Euskal Herriari	To the Basque Country
Semetxo asko dauzka	Many sons
Debruak uguri	Has the devil
Izan zaitez bada aren	Please may there also be
Gurizon zaindari	Protectors for all of us
Fidegabe guzti hil erazi	Kill all the infidels

Hara! Father Itcea grinned at the last line that appeared as if on its own. A fitting reminder that God could strike people down at any time.

The priest folded the paper with the verses into an envelope. If he hurried, he could make it to the newspaper office before Mass, and it could be printed in the afternoon edition.

A second robin joined the first in song. Today was going to be a good day. Father Itcea would mention Blanca's vision in his morning homilies, and by the time the parishioners had their midday meal, his "anonymous" verses would be published. Who wouldn't want to go to Aranzibia Hill after that?

He opened his front door. There stood Blanca's mother, Maider, her face aglow but her hands shaking.

"Aita Itcea, I come to beg forgiveness for my lack of faith." Maider's voice trembled as her words poured out. "The Blessed Mother has chosen my Blanca as her messenger, and I did not believe . . . that the Virgin appears to Blanca, born to such an unworthy woman as me!"

Father Itcea gently led Maider inside the rectory. "I understand—" he began, but she would not be interrupted.

"—It's exactly as my mother had foretold." Maider's words kept coming fast, in Basque and French. "My whole life she said she would help bring forth a new saint, and I thought she meant Bernadette of Soubirous."

Maider took a breath as Father Itcea put a hand on her shoulder. "As did I," he said. "I see now Blanca might be the saint we seek." No point in mentioning that Maria Gurrutxetegia had also been a candidate.

"That is my hope as well." A look of relief washed over Maider's face. "I thought it was prideful to think the Blessed Mother would look with such favor on the daughter of a woman like me, such a sinner . . ."

Her eyes brimmed with tears.

Father Itcea did not know what sins she referred to, for he never pried outside the confessional.

"We are all sinners," he said. "As the Virgin Mary told Blanca . . . this is why she has come, to cleanse us of our sins and bring us back to her Son, Jesus Christ."

The clock chimed quarter to seven. It was too late now to deliver his verses to the paper before Mass. He would have to wait until tomorrow's edition.

"Do you want to wait here until I return?" Father Itcea said kindly.

Maider bowed her head and took the seat he offered her.

As he left the rectory, Father Itcea remembered how skeptical Bernadette's parents had been at first. Once they believed, they became their daughter's most adamant supporters, then the masses poured in to see Bernadette in vision and the miracles and healings multiplied.

If Maider were to stand beside Blanca while she was in vision, perhaps the same thing would happen on Aranzibia Hill.

* * *

I down another shot of whiskey, Old Simon's visage blurring. I don't care. I had come so close to seeing Caireann, only to have the door slammed in my face by her husband. I tap my empty glass and drink up the whiskey as soon as Old Simon pours it.

Caireann was so lovely, so sweet. Surely she could have married anyone she wanted once she rejected me? I still remember the looks of envy shot my way by other young men when they saw us together. When she didn't respond to my letters, I'd assumed that our romance had meant less to her than it had to me. And now to learn she'd married not only a man old enough to be her father but also one clearly unable to give her the lifestyle to which she'd been accustomed. To which she was entitled.

"Simon!" I say. "Another!"

A young man takes the barstool beside me.

"May I join you?"

"Ah, Cruz!" I shake his hand. "Of course!" He has grown quite tall since my arrival to Indartze.

Old Simon asks for our order.

"Two coffees, please." Cruz puts pesetas on the counter.

"It's good to see you," I begin. "I've been wanting to talk to you about something." This feels true, but my head throbs as I try to remember what that something is.

"I've been meaning to talk to you myself," Cruz says. "I wanted to thank you, on behalf of my family, for helping me bring my sister home safely the other day. And to apologize for my father's rudeness."

The coffees come and I sip mine, though Cruz's words have already made me feel better.

"I hope your sister's doing well," I say.

"She is," Cruz says. "Between Remedios and my mother, they figured out the treatment she needed."

Old Simon takes my shot glass away and replaces it with a glass of water.

"Our grandmother-that-was had epilepsy, and I guess Blanca has it as well," Cruz says. "That's why she's having seizures and hallucinations. Ama thinks Blanca is having visions of the Virgin Mary." Here, Cruz's tone turns as sarcastic as the voice in my head that I suppress in my professional quest to be impartial.

"That would explain a lot," I say. Does Cruz know I was present at Blanca's "vision" in the church? I drink my coffee slowly as I consider what to divulge.

"Aita Itcea has worked my mother into a frenzy about the whole thing," he says. "He's convinced her that Blanca's been chosen by the Virgin Mary for a great mission. Not only for the people of Indartze but for the whole world." Cruz's gray eyes flash with anger. "Now that my sister's feeling better, he's persuaded my mother to let Blanca go up Aranzibia Hill every day, with him there to translate the Virgin's messages into Spanish and French."

"Oh no!" I put a Gaulois to my lips and offer him one. "That means the Virgin will say whatever Father Itcea wants her to say."

"And my mother." Cruz exhales, taking the cigarette with his left hand. "She insists on going with them every time. To 'protect my daughter's reputation,' she says."

Although not altogether sober, I'm impressed with the boy. He's trying to shield his sister from religious fanatics without condemning his mother as one.

"I'm sure your mother's doing what she feels is right," I say. "But this could easily get out of control. Is there anything I can do to help?"

"There is," Cruz replies. "I got to know you when you first came to town because you would come here each night playing your songs and learning ours." He takes out a piece of paper from his pocket. The glint of his pewter pocket watch catches my eye. Cruz tucks the timepiece away and hands the paper to me. "I wrote down what's happening to Blanca, warning people her visions are manipulated." He looks down, as I used to do when embarrassed. "My friend . . . Sofia . . . translated them for me into Castilian. If you were to set the words to music and sing the verses in here, perhaps that would convince the people of Indartze not to believe everything they hear."

"Good idea!" I wonder from Old Simon's expression if I'm speaking too loudly.

A patron takes a seat at the bar, unfurling today's *Le Matin* to read as he drinks.

And that's another way I can get your message out, I say under my breath in English so he won't understand.

CHAPTER TWENTY

Blanca awoke to her cat's meows. Xuriko was playing in the bedsheets, ready to start the day. As was Blanca, even though she'd been up late on Aranzibia Hill, praying the Rosary and listening to the petitions of the pilgrims.

"I just listen to what's in people's hearts," she told Xuriko. "And that makes them feel better." The cat nuzzled Blanca's neck and purred.

Last night's vigil had exhausted Blanca. After a long visitation from the Blessed Mother—Ama said it lasted thirty minutes, though it felt like no time at all—the people came to her with their petitions. They asked for the Blessed Mother's intercession on behalf of family members they feared were stuck in purgatory; for forgiveness for their own sins, too unspeakable to specify; to plead that ill or injured friends find relief from their suffering. Some people simply brought photos of their loved ones or rosaries for Blanca to bless with a kiss. Ama translated for those who spoke only French. To make sure the crowds could not rush the "vision platform," Refugic had put up a chain-link fence around it.

It was exhausting and exhilarating. Blanca found the words that provided comfort or the gesture to sooth the suffering souls. She knew the Blessed Mother gave her these simple words and gestures, just as she used Blanca to deliver her divine messages. Blanca didn't always remember what the Blessed Mother said, though, and last night's visitation was a blur, so Father Itcea wrote it all down.

Every day *Gure Txoko* reported bigger and bigger crowds. Last night, the priest estimated that thousands of people had come.

Xuriko played with a rosary from Blanca's end table.

"Now, now, little one." Blanca gently took her grandmother's red beads from the kitty's paws. "Let's not disrespect the Blessed Mother."

The cat jumped from the bed. Blanca had been too tired to change after coming home from Aranzibia Hill early this morning, so she smoothed her hair and dress before following her cat to the kitchen. The smell of *kafesnea* and bacon filled the air, and Blanca beamed at the happy scene. Ama, Aita, and Cruz were sitting together at the table eating omelets and offerings given Blanca by her petitioners: *jamón serrano* from Madrid and Catalan *mató* cheese from Barcelona. Tins of *foie gras* and *pâté* sat on the cupboard next to jars of red peppers from Ezpeleta and bottles of wine from la Rioja.

"Good morning!" Blanca said. "Everything smells delicious!" So much better than the water and day-old bread they used to have.

"I saved some for you." Her mother smiled broadly, setting a plate next to Cruz. He winked at her and squeezed her hand. Ama gave her a cup of coffee-with-milk and a white chocolate bonbon from *Chocolat Cazenave*, as Amatxi Angeline used to do.

Once Father Itcea learned how much Blanca loved these candies, he brought them from Bayonne himself. He'd done whatever he could to promote her visions and protect her from the skeptics. He was a good man and a good priest.

Blanca did so much talking on Aranzibia Hill every night that her family left her undisturbed in the mornings. She liked that they discussed normal, everyday things. They seemed to make a point of avoiding disagreements. Though Cruz clearly did not believe in Blanca's visions, he did not argue the point.

"I care about how people act, not what they believe," he'd say. Blanca knew he'd gotten this idea from Sofia.

"Will you pass the bread, Aita?" Blanca waited for a break in the conversation to ask.

"*Hemen dun.* Here you are." Aita's hand shook as he handed her the basket. He seemed to be losing weight, though they had more food than ever before.

Blanca felt a pang of guilt that she hadn't noticed Aita's worsening health. She would make a point of praying to the Blessed Mother for him, especially whenever she went to Aranzibia Hill.

"Thank you, Aita." Blanca reached for his hand and it felt cool to the touch, even though he sat close to the fire. This worried her. She would give him bigger doses of Sabine's spring water.

The mahogany mantle clock chimed eight. Doña Carmen had given Blanca the clock, as well as the Deluxe Zenith radio beside it, in gratitude for bringing the people back to the One True Faith. Sharing these presents with her family made Blanca happy.

Cruz adjusted the dial until he found his daily news program. The show was in Castilian, so they had to be very quiet and pay close attention. Blanca liked the new words and information she'd learned this way.

Good morning, fellow citizens. Here are the headlines for Thursday, the twenty-eighth of May, nineteen thirty-one. The Republican Cabinet has decided to seize all the private property of former king Alfonso. The ultimate decision about disposal of the property will be made when the National Assembly convenes.

"Por fin!" Cruz clenched his fist. "It's about time!"
Ama made the sign of the cross.
Aita sighed heavily.

An inquiry will also take up accusations that the former king was party to a plot to incite the riots of the past few days as a means of discrediting the republic...

"Liars!" Ama said. "Our king would never do such a thing!"
"I wouldn't be so sure," Cruz shot back. "What has he ever done for people like us?"
"Aski!" Aita tapped his walking stick. "That's enough!"
"Let's not fight," Blanca intervened, her morning now spoiled. "Can't we turn that off and eat in peace?"
Cruz turned the radio up instead.

It was decided to take means to protect the public interest. Martial law has been declared throughout Spain today. Cordons of soldiers were drawn up around the Bank of Spain to fight off a threatened attack by lawbreakers...

Transgresores—the word hung in the air before Blanca.
"Who are they calling 'lawbreakers'?" Cruz turned off the radio. "People fighting against unfair laws?"
Anxiety overwhelmed Blanca with a memory from last night's vision.
Cruz took a cigarette from his shirt pocket, struck a match against his leather sole to light it, and put it between his lips. "Guess I'm a lawbreaker."
He stormed out and Blanca held back tears, for she remembered now what the Blessed Mother had said last night. She'd prophesied that in seven days' time violators of God's laws would be struck down.

Father Itcea swelled with pride at the spiritual bounty his efforts had wrought. Thousands of people beheld Blanca as she stood in the living shrine that Aranzibia Hill had become. No roof but the immaculate vault of heaven, no walls but the surrounding mountains, no sound but the prayers issued from fervent hearts. Refugio's four beautifully carved beams stood amid the four oak trees, and worshippers gathered around the altar from all sides. Inspired, he hoped, by his accounts at daily Mass of the throngs who honored Our Lady at Lourdes, the supplicants had brought small gifts to festoon this holy place. Paper hearts with "Blessed are you" or "Pray for us" written on them in a child's hand, sometimes accompanied by rudimentary drawings of the Virgin Mary or Blanca, and rosaries and red rose petals dotted the linen altar cloth that had originally belonged to Maider's mother.

The pilgrims' devotion brought Father Itcea to tears. People he knew to be of modest means came dressed in their Sunday best. Men removed their hats or berets upon summiting Aranzibia Hill; women veiled their faces with mantillas. Adolescent girls, and even boys, clutched prayer books against their chests.

Most impressive of all were the ladies who'd occupied the front pews at Our Lady of Sorrows at daily Mass since Father Itcea had arrived in Indartze, murmuring their criticism of him to each other under the guise of prayer, he was sure of it. Led by Doña Carmen, they knelt on the rocky ground before Blanca as soon as the daily ritual began at five o'clock until the girl's visions concluded, sometimes well past midnight. Neither he nor any of the other worshippers could withstand the pain of kneeling for so long.

Nor, it seemed, could the skepticism of the nonbelievers withstand the vehemence of the believers. Cruz and William no longer came.

The bells at Our Lady of Sorrows tolled five, and Father Itcea grasped his black stone rosary. "May the miracle come today," he prayed to himself. "I have done all I can, Blessed Mother. May it come today."

Blanca stepped onto the platform, her mother right behind her. The faithful hushed one another and kneeled, many of them on copies of the very newspapers where the priest's "anonymous" verses had appeared daily, announcing Blanca's visions and the miracle the Virgin Mary had promised. Father Itcea glanced at the couple beside him. Dust coated their clothes and mud covered their shoes; under their knees was *Le Matin*. He realized he had seen them here each day this week. If they could patiently await the miracle, so could he.

A white dove swooped down and perched on Blanca's shoulder for a moment, as if the Virgin Mary herself wished to confer her blessing on the child.

Onlookers cried out.

Two elderly women approached Father Itcea on their knees. "Bless you, Aita Itcea. Now we believe!" They lifted the hem of his robe, kissing it.

He took their hands in his, too moved to speak. To think that he had brought these women back to the Church! He'd broadcast Blanca's visions, the people had come, and many would be saved.

Then humility swept over him. He was merely an instrument in the unfolding of the miracle, whatever it might be. He'd realized that pride as much as piety had motivated his promotion of Blanca's visions. He'd wanted to be feted as the priest who'd made her divine prophecies known, to take credit for the resurgence in faith the apparitions would surely foment.

In the weeks since Blanca's nightly visions had begun, he had realized the Virgin Mary had her own purposes for her visitations. Peace and joy filled his whole being during these ceremonies, and he rediscovered the pure faith in God that had drawn him to the priesthood. Feeling ashamed of the arrogance and snobbery he'd often felt toward his parishioners, he now dedicated himself to accepting whatever role the Blessed Mother might give him in bringing about the promised miracle.

And the role seemed to be to record the girl's words. Father Itcea took out a notebook and pencil from his pocket. Rain often accompanied the Virgin Mary's visits, and he had learned the hard way that the ink from his fine-tipped pens bled on the paper, rendering his notes illegible.

Blanca bowed her head to Father Itcea.

Raising his right hand high to silence the crowd, he made the sign of the cross and said, "Let us pray." Then he gestured toward Maider to lead the opening song to the Virgin Mary. Male and female voices from the gathering joined in the hymn.

Agur Maria graziaz betea	Hail Mary full of grace
Jauna da zurekin	The Lord is with you
Benedikatua zare	Blessed are you
Emazte guzien artean	Among women
Eta benedikatua da	And blessed is the fruit
Zure sabeleko fruitua Jesus	Of your womb Jesus

As Father Itcea joined in, he felt a deep connection with his fellow singers, a connection to a purpose higher than his own. Why had he been unable to create such a feeling during Mass?

Maria Saindua	Holy Mary
Jainkoaren Ama	Mother of God
Egizu otoitz gu bekatorosentzat	Pray for us sinners
Orai eta gure	Now and at the hour
Heriotzeko orenean	Of our death
Halabiz	Amen

After the song ended, the multitude fell silent.

"Let us pray for the souls of the departed," Blanca said. Refugio brought the jeweled box containing slips of paper with the names. It was one of the sixteenth-century church vessels stolen from Our Lady of Sorrows, then recovered by Refugio. The anger Father Itcea had felt when he first learned of the robbery rose again, then subsided. He'd been outraged that anyone would steal from the church. Now he could think of no holier place for Father Zabaleta's valuable Eucharistic items to be reconsecrated. This modest chapel held more spiritual power than the most majestic cathedral.

Blanca took out a slip of paper and read the name on it aloud. After a short silence, she kissed the piece of paper and handed it back to Refugio, who found a place for it among the rosaries and rose petals, creating a beautiful bouquet of offerings on the altar.

When this part of the ritual was done, Blanca gingerly closed the lid of the jeweled box and gave it to Refugio. Then, as Father Itcea had suggested she do, Blanca wrapped her grandmother Angeline's red rosary around her fingers so that everyone could see it. Angeline had been such a devotee of Bernadette Soubirous at Lourdes, he felt it was important to have a religious artifact linking the two apparition sites.

Blanca's sweet voice interrupted his musings. "Are there others who need our prayers?" She asked this each afternoon so that those who couldn't write could offer their names as well.

Refugio spoke first, as had become the tradition.

"For the soul of Antonio."

Even though it had been over a year since his father had died, Refugio could not say the name without his voice cracking. Father Itcea wondered at the transformation the Virgin Mary had wrought in him. He had grown into an exemplar of faith and humility respected by all. Once a despised *agota* cowering in the shadows in dirty shirts and torn pants, Refugio now stood tall and proud in his slightly worn but impeccably maintained suits.

The priest's eyes welled and he let the tears fall, though for another Antonio. When his brother died, Father Itcea had been so preoccupied with studying casuistry and Mariology that he'd neglected his feelings.

"For my mother, Pilarcho," a woman said. "*Goian bego.*"

"May she rest in peace." Blanca led the gathering in the refrain.

Silence buffered the petition, then a man said, "For my aunt Katalin." He choked out the name.

"May she rest in peace," Blanca mouthed the words so that the faithful could hear each other's prayers.

Father Itcea closed his eyes and brought to mind his own devout mother, dead ten years. He'd never properly grieved her either. The tears came again.

The reciting of the names came faster and faster from farther down Aranzibia Hill. With each stranger's name mentioned came the memory of a departed person close to Father Itcea: his father, his grandmother, his older sister, his spiritual director. As the litany of petitions rose more faintly from farther down the hill, so too did vague images of women unknown to Father Itcea appear: a woman about Maider's age with arresting blue eyes; a well-dressed woman with fiery red hair; and a young girl several years older than Blanca, her face radiant as she looked toward heaven, citing Psalm 37's exhortation to "wait a little while, and the wicked will be no more."

These strangers, too, comforted him. He felt a mysterious, powerful kinship with them.

He opened his eyes. A single cloud appeared in the blue sky, and Father Itcea was impressed at the Virgin Mary's cleverness. She'd manifested an obvious reference, from Hebrews, to the "cloud of witnesses" or communion of saints. Perhaps these unknown women prayed for him in heaven as these pilgrims prayed with him on earth, all of them accompanying him on his journey toward God, hoping one day to welcome him to Paradise.

CHAPTER TWENTY-ONE

B lanca opened her bedroom shutters to welcome the sunshine. A perfect day to celebrate Corpus Christi! Many children would make their First Holy Communion at Our Lady of Sorrows today, as she had done two years ago. There would be a beautiful procession around the plaza afterward, then the families would give out treats to those assembled. Yet that's not why Blanca was excited. The Blessed Mother had told her the true meaning of the holy day—that "we are all the Body of Christ" and that Blanca herself would help bring about this beautiful vision of the Church.

The celebration came about because of a saint named Juliana of Liege. An orphan who lived with a community of women taking care of lepers, Juliana became devoted to the Blessed Sacrament, the idea that the Eucharist was actually the body and blood of Jesus, not just a symbol. Saint Juliana petitioned bishops for forty years to dedicate a feast day to it. One bishop eventually became pope and established the Feast of Corpus Christi.

"We all build the Church together," the Blessed Mother had told Blanca. "By caring for the sick and lonely, by making sacrifices for others, and by loving each other, we all become the Body of Christ."

Blanca loved this idea of the Church and was thrilled to learn a woman had played such an essential role in bringing forth an important feast. Maybe Blanca was helping people by sharing with them the Blessed Mother's messages, even though she didn't always understand them.

Juliana had had confusing visions too, like the full moon shining on a church with a dark spot on it.

Lately, more and more of the ill and dying had come to Blanca for healing. The more people came, the more water flowed from Sabine's spring. Sabine's water really seemed to help them, so Blanca had taken more of the spring water home herself. Though it brought relief to Aita's aching knees, he still struggled walking up and down the steps.

The smell of frying bacon wafted into her room. Blanca followed the savory smell into the kitchen.

"*Egun on*, Aita —good morning!" Blanca hugged her father from behind as he stood at the stove.

He tried to smile but grimaced instead.

"*Barkatu*—I'm sorry." She forgot Aita's back had also been bothering him. She worried he was getting so weak.

"Let me finish that." Blanca took the fork from her father. "And maybe you can use Sabine's spring water afterward?"

Aita sat down at the table's head. An oak chair now sat where a rickety wicker chair used to be, a gift Blanca had bought him with the donations from the pilgrims.

After the bacon got crispy, she fried two fresh eggs—more offerings—in the bacon grease.

"Here you go." Blanca put the platter and two plates on the table. She reached onto a higher shelf for glasses when she noticed a large book pressed against the back. Standing on tiptoe, she could barely reach its yellowed pages.

I wondered where this was. She looked at the etching on the cover with the hideous goat-monster and the naked girl on the mountain. The drawing use to frighten her because the grove resembled the one on Aranzibia Hill. Now she realized only good things happened on the apparition site. The devil was nowhere to be found.

"What's that?" asked Aita.

"It's that book of folktales Ama brought home from Amatxi Angeline's." She held the book carefully, remembering it was very old.

Aita wiped his hands, then held them out to Blanca. "Let me see."

As she handed over the book, Blanca glanced at the cave on the cover. It reminded her of one of the stories her mother had read to her.

"Ah, the book all her stories come from," Aita said.

"Yes, Ama used to read to me after Amatxi died, until my visions really started coming," Blanca said. It felt good to talk to Aita so freely about this.

"It's interesting how things come full circle." Aita took Blanca's hand and laid it along with his own on the book of folktales, reverently, as if it were the Bible. "Your mother's ancestor Sabine Elizalde wrote this book. She was also a teacher and great friend to my relative Maria."

"Sabine of the healing spring?" Blanca asked. "We found a tablet dedicated to her and made it the cornerstone of the altar." She hoped Aita would be able to go up Aranzibia Hill one day to see it for himself.

"The very same," he said. "I'd forgotten all about the spring. It hadn't flowed for years and years. And then you started having your visions . . ." He trailed off. "Your mother and brother have gone into town already?"

"Yes, Aita," Blanca said.

"Then it's a good time to tell you the whole story of Maria." He touched the garnet pendant around her neck. "And how her spirit lives on in you."

The bells of Our Lady of Sorrows struck ten. Blanca would have to leave soon to make it in time for the Corpus Christi procession.

She stayed put, though. The true blessing was right here.

The shouts from the street outside my window intensify the pounding of my hangover, jolting me awake.

"*Nueva España!* A New Spain!"

My ears perk up. I haven't heard political grumblings for many days, lost in my drunken fugue. I draw back the flimsy curtains and look outside. A crowd marches its way toward the center of Indartze. Sofia leads, her thick hair swept away from her face and cascading over her shoulders. She holds her chin up, making her seem taller than I know her to be. She holds a sign saying *Enseñanza libre y laica!*—Free secular education! Cruz follows closely at heel, loudly echoing Sofia's chants: "*Nueva España! Nueva España!*" The throng following her includes perhaps two dozen people, their attire ranging from work clothes to Sunday best. Some wave the red Communist flag inscribed with the yellow hammer and sickle. Others hold aloft the purple, yellow, and red banner of the Second Spanish Republic. Still others carry the Union Jack, but in red, white, and green, the Basque *ikurriña*.

The mix of political symbols makes my heart jump. I stand close to the window to get a better look. The assembly reminds me of the multitude who'd cheered Sofia's speech in favor of women's suffrage at Bar Herria: men and women, ranging in age from about twenty to early sixties. This time, children join their parents, the youngsters wearing red sashes around their waists or red five-pointed stars stamped with yellow sickles affixed to their shirts. One little girl carries a doll draped in a red sash.

I don't see Michel, Sofia's stalwart sentry. I last saw him on Aranzibia Hill, kneeling before Blanca while in vision. Does he now believe?

"*Adelante!*" The shouts come again. "Onward and forward!"

Ignoring the churning in my stomach from last night's drinks, I throw on some clothes, put a pack of Gauloises in my shirt pocket next to my notebook and pen, and rush down the stairs. I'll follow a few steps behind Sofia and the demonstrators, without getting too involved.

Thunder claps outside, and storm clouds merge overhead. I wonder whether I should get my hat. A percussive beat from the pack pulls me forward. A young man marches with a large drum poised at a perpendicular angle to his waist, thudding the sheepskin head with a wool-tipped stick. I saw such drums in the French army's bugle corps during the Great War. Instead of the bright red caps of the soldier, this boy wears the navy blue beret, signifying the equality of all men.

"*Patria sin Iglesia!* Country without Church!" Sofia leads her followers in the slogan. Cruz shouts with particular enthusiasm, raising his fist.

Thunder syncopates with the drum. Other protesters take up Cruz's motto, alternating from Basque to Castilian, as we near the plaza. What I see stops me in my tracks.

There in the middle of the square stands Caireann, leading a group of children in song. Despite her graying hair and wrinkles, the image of the young woman I'd fallen in love with peeks through. Her radiant smile and contagious laughter. The sun-kissed cheeks; those marvelous seeking eyes. The ache in my heart deepens. The beautiful life we could have had if I'd not left her!

The sun pierces the storm clouds and shines on Caireann. A half dozen children stand before her. The boys wear suits and ties. The girls have donned long white dresses and veils, and they hold small baskets. I recognize this prelude to a First Holy Communion. Caireann raises her baton, and the children sing along with her.

Cantemos al amore de los amores
Let us sing to the love above all loves

Cantemos al Señor
Let us sing to the Lord

The children's angelic voices coupled with Caireann's pure soprano transport me to a place of beauty and tranquility. Sofia's followers stand silently, as if hypnotized. Doña Carmen strolls into the plaza. Dressed in a brocade black silk dress, she wears an elaborate mantilla and the largest crucifix pendant I have ever seen. Its crowned tips look as sharp as daggers.

At Caireann's cue the girls take rose petals from their baskets and sprinkle them onto the pavement.

Gloria a Cristo Jesús, Cielos y tierra
Glory be to Jesus Christ, heaven and earth

Bendecid al Señor, Honor y Gloria a Ti
Bless the Lord, Honor and Glory to You

Villagers spill out from the homes and cafes lining the square. Before many residences stand temporary altars, low tables covered with handmade linens on top of which lie small crucifixes or plastic holy water receptacles shaped in the image of the Virgin Mary. Beside the church, a pile of bricks sits alongside a neat stack of two-by-fours, for the church restoration in progress.

Amor para siempre por Ti, Dios del amor
Love forever to You, God of Love

"God of love?" Cruz breaks the spell. "Love of the rich, you mean!"

Caireann fixes Cruz with the fiery stare she used to shoot at me whenever we had a row. He blushes, looks down, then glares at his mother. He stands with his right arm bowed outward from his hip, his thin lips pursed in a straight line.

"*Patria sin Iglesia!*" Cruz raises his fist again and his voice echoes against the buildings. "Country without Church!"

"*Arriba España moderna!*" Sofia takes Cruz's hand. "Here's to a modern Spain!"

"How dare you speak such blasphemy!" Doña Carmen shouts back.

A wind kicks up from the north, knocking the mantilla off her head. She glowers at a boy beside her, who runs after it.

"*Escuela sí, catecismo no!*" Sofia approaches Doña Carmen. "Yes to school! No to catechism!"

Her followers take up the motto. Onlookers stand agape.

Doña Carmen gives Sofia a look that could only be described as *mal de ojo*—the evil eye.

Sofia tightens her grip on Cruz's hand, raises her voice even louder. "*Patria sin Iglesia!*" She looks at Doña Carmen without flinching.

"Country without Church!" The chant echoes across the plaza as Sofia's followers take it up, louder with each repetition.

Caireann raises her baton, says something to the children in Basque, and leads them in a new verse of their song. Spectators join in.

Unamos nuestra voz a los cantares
We unite our voices to the singers

Del coro celestial
Of the celestial choir

Verse and chant battle for dominance. Everyone gives voice to one or the other, vehemence animating their expressions. The devout and disbelievers eye each other suspiciously. The girls stop scattering their rose petals. A few boys look ready to cry.

Cruz stares at the entrance of Our Lady of Sorrows, and I follow his gaze. There stands Father Itcea, wearing the red vestments of Corpus Christi, symbolizing Christ's sacrificing himself on the cross for all sinners. He grips a shiny monstrance, large enough that even from the edge of the plaza, I can see the rubies and emeralds encrusted in the silver.

"Why does our priest need such jewels?" Sofia points an accusing finger at Father Itcea. "Won't he serve God more by selling them and giving the money to the poor?"

Nods and exclamations indicate I am not alone in concurring with Sofia.

"What do you know about serving God?" Caireann yells back, a malevolence in her voice I have never heard. "You witch, turning my son against the Church! Against me!"

An enigmatic expression on his face, Father Itcea raises a hand as if to speak. The multitude chimes in before he can do so.

"Everything was fine here until Sofia turned up!"

"How dare she speak against the Church!"

"She'll go to hell for that!"

Doña Carmen, her mantilla askew on her head, raises her hands and looks up to the sky. "May God strike down the infidel!"

Thunder roars as the clock tower strikes noon. Crows escape the belfry.

The priest raises his arms to regain the mob's attention. I feel he will say something momentous. The electricity among the onlookers is palpable. The flesh on my arms prickles.

Then lightning flashes, striking Father Itcea's left hand. The bolt burns a ragged line through his vestment to his chest. His face as white as the Communion host, he opens his mouth to speak. Another clap of thunder renders him inaudible.

Indistinct screams burst from the plaza. Crying children run toward Caireann, who shelters them in her arms. She drops her baton, and it rolls toward Father Itcea. Some protesters cower; others try to direct the swarm away from the church. Sofia runs toward the priest, as do I.

Father Itcea staggers, his face contorts. He struggles to hold his monstrance high. It wavers.

Thunder roars overhead, sounding like huge boulders crashing down. Lightning flashes again, hitting the monstrance. His face more crimson than his robes, Father Itcea clutches his chest and stumbles down the stone steps.

His head hits the pavement, and Sofia kneels beside him. I reach him shortly thereafter. She feels for a pulse at his neck, then shakes her head. I listen to his chest.

"He's gone," I say, surprised to see her eyes welling.

I touch Father Itcea's arm and wince at the burn there. No blood blemishes his skin, suggesting his heart stopped immediately after the lightning struck.

"He looks peaceful," whispers Sofia.

I nod. The priest's eyes stare up, the sudden blue of the sky reflected there. A mysterious smile lies upon his lips. The hand holding the monstrance is now fused to it, the fingers twisted in a grotesque manner.

The crowd gathers around Father Itcea's body, Sofia and me, but people stand a respectful distance away. Some men silently take off their berets and hats, others weep openly. Women stand stoically, clutching at rosaries or children; others sway back and forth, keening.

"She killed him!" Doña Carmen's voice booms. "She pricked him with her fingernail and poisoned him!"

My pulse quickens in alarm. "No, the lightning struck him down." I move closer to Sofia.

"This is what happens when a woman dares to preach such blasphemies!" Doña Carmen's face is contorted with rage. "She brings the wrath of God upon us!"

Unfamiliar voices chime in:

"Murderer!"

"*Sorgina!*"

"Witch!"

"She must be punished!" Doña Carmen lunges at Sofia, and others follow suit.

Sofia stands up and I rise with her, the priest's dead body at our feet. Cruz rushes toward her. A chromed stainless steel and pewter pocket watch engraved with the Celtic Tree of Life falls out of his pocket. Stunned by what this reveals, I stall momentarily in my defense of Sofia.

She waves us off.

"Let them do what they will," she says, calm determination on her face. "Let them see what zealotry breeds."

Doña Carmen raises her Bible and viciously beats Sofia about the face with it. Its hard leather spine lands on Sofia's temples and eyes over and over, and she falls.

Suddenly Old Simon appears. He wrests the Bible from Doña Carmen as she raises it again. "Carmen, *querida*! What in God's name are you doing?" He looks at her, pleadingly.

Her eyes glare back at him. She shakes him off, yanks her pendant off its chain, and plunges the crucifix into Sofia's mouth. I scream as Cruz tackles Doña Carmen. Too late. Sofia's lifeless body lies beside Father Itcea's, blood gushing from her lips.

Doña Carmen scrambles to her feet, her nostrils dilating like those of a war-horse. She directs others to attack us, and they do not hesitate. They grab bricks and plywood, use fists and shepherd's crooks. I'm too shocked at what's happened to Sofia—why didn't her followers help her?—to defend myself. Epithets and screams pound against my ears as my head throbs and my knees buckle under the blows. A knife blade cuts my cheek as I fall. I cry out in agony. I reach up, despite my disbelief, hoping for divine intervention. The last thing I see before I lose consciousness is the belfry of Our Lady of Sorrows. Engulfed in flames.

As she reached the summit of Aranzibia Hill, Blanca thought about what Aita had told her, how her brave relative Maria, only fifteen at the time, had stood up to the Inquisition even as flames consumed her. How Sabine taught Maria to read and to make healing potions, and how she did everything she could to protect her against false accusations of witchcraft. Even after Maria's death, Sabine worked with the parish priest Salvador Zabaleta to clear her name. The reliquary pendant containing Maria's ashes cool against her neck, Blanca beamed as she thought of the goodness and bravery of ordinary people like those of Indartze.

She approached the altar. All around it sunflowers had grown. Blanca loved how they always tilted toward the sun. The sun peeked through the gray clouds and shone on the plaque dedicated to Sabine hundreds of years ago, now the gathering place for so many good people praying to the Blessed Mother on behalf of their loved ones.

Today was the perfect day to give thanks to her in their name and to her ancestors who'd done good things in their lives—good that might have been passed on to Blanca in ways she didn't realize.

Perhaps the Blessed Mother would have a message for her today about how she might continue this family legacy. Maybe she would appear if Blanca came all by herself, as she had the first time Blanca saw her. Here on this mountain, where Sabine had lived, where the Blessed Mother had first appeared to her, on this special feast day.

Blanca lay down on the plywood Refugio had placed around the altar. The grass between the planks tickled her arms, stretched out straight and wide, as though awaiting an embrace from heaven. She kept her eyes closed, for the light from above was bright. She breathed in short puffs, taking in the scent of roses that filled Aranzibia Hill. The bright light pushed against Blanca's eyelids and tingled all the way to her toes, as if filling her whole body with sunshine.

Blanca's face warmed; she smiled as a breeze wafted through the grove. She could tell her cheeks were as rosy as the petals now falling gently on her skin. She pushed up the sleeves of her coat and dress so that she could better feel the soft touch of the Blessed Mother, for that's what the petals were. Blanca's pulse beat so hard, she felt sure her heart would jump out of her chest. She forced her lids open and saw doves fluttering before her eyes. Then her lids fell shut, for the brightness was too great. Her breathing slowed.

A crow cawed in the oak grove, and the sound rose to a crescendo as other crows joined in.

Then the message came.

"Soon there will be a time of great trial."

This was not what Blanca expected.

"I am listening, Ama Maite Maria." Blanca's body grew stiff.

"A battle will come where brother will fight brother. Where husband will separate from wife. Where friend will become foe."

A heaviness clutched Blanca's heart.

"The righteous will eventually triumph, and the wicked will be exorcised from these lands."

Blanca noticed the word *gaizkatu*, as in the Blessed Mother's first message. Did she mean Blanca should help her get rid of evil people? Did this include her family and friends?

"At first, many Basques will suffer. A horrific new weapon will drop from the sky and kill thousands of innocent people."

Please, no! Blanca strained to open her eyes and plead for the safety of these unknown innocents. Tears streamed down her face.

"The righteous must stay steadfast. They will look to you for strength."

Me? Blanca's lips trembled at the words she longed to say but could not. She didn't think she had enough strength to carry out such a big mission. So far, she'd mostly helped the Blessed Mother heal people and deliver her messages. She'd thought her mission was to get rid of their worries, their illnesses . . .

"A false prophet will rule Spain for many years. He will clothe himself in the white garments of the lamb, though he be a wolf."

"What can I do?" Blanca pleaded.

"You must give your people hope during those dark times."

Blanca knew she'd grown up since her visions had started coming months ago, but this request was too much. "Wouldn't a man of God like Aita Itcea be more capable of carrying out this task?"

"He has played his part. It is up to you now. Just do as I say, and you will know what to do when your time comes, as did your ancestor, Maria."

But Maria burned at the stake!

Sweat dampened Blanca's skin and her body grew warm. The air felt sultry and close, making it hard for her to breath. Was this how Maria felt as her pyre was set on fire? Did the Blessed Mother mean for her to suffer like that? She wouldn't be able to endure it . . .

A driving wind blew through the grove from the north, then Blanca felt the Blessed Mother's smile on her cheeks, like a kiss. She opened her eyes to see her face, framed with long flaxen hair. Wearing a flowing gown of cornflower blue, the Blessed Mother had the most beautiful smile. Blanca felt seen, for all that she was, for the first time in her life.

All worry and fear left her. The Blessed Mother trusted her to carry out this important mission, so she would find the strength. After all, the Blessed Mother had once felt unworthy of her destiny too. And she was the Mother of God; she would know what was best.

The crows fell silent. The white doves surrounded Blanca, serenading her with their low, sweet song.

The Blessed Mother held out her hand to Blanca.

"I am your servant." Blanca took the Blessed Mother's hand. "Let it be done to me according to your will." She grasped the memorial pendant and felt the bravery Maria and Sabine must have had as they met their destinies, no matter the cost to themselves, pursuing what was right and true, as the Blessed Mother asked Blanca to do. Blanca smiled; she would trust her to show the way.

And she surrendered into her dazzling light.

This novel is loosely based on events that transpired between 1931 and 1933 in the Basque Country of northern Spain. My main source material is William Christian's excellent account, *Visionaries: The Spanish Republic and the Reign of Christ* (1996), which appeared to me in a bin outside a university bookstore. As Christian demonstrates, the early 1930s brought political, social, and religious tumult to Spain. The election on April 12, 1931, ushered in the Second Republic. King Alfonso XIII fled the country, leaving Spain without a Bourbon monarch for the first time since 1700. The new Constitution promised to separate Church and State, extend the vote to women as well as men, provide free secular education to girls and boys, allow for civil marriages, and permit divorce, thus scandalizing the Catholic elites that had ruled Spain for centuries. Rioters burned down churches and convents; protesters and priests alike absconded with valuable church objects to keep them safe or melt them down for precious metals.

On June 29, 1931, a 7-year-old girl and her 9-year-old brother claimed the Virgin Mary had appeared to them in the small town of Ezkioga in the province of Gipuzkoa. Soon thereafter, other Basques—mostly children and young women—claimed that the Virgin Mary appeared to them as well. The Virgin Mary's messages ran the gamut from simple exhortations to pray the rosary daily to the more challenging (and enigmatic) charge to "liberate Spain" ("*gaizkatu España*"). Miracles and Chastisements were foretold.

The most famous (or infamous) of these seers was a 9-year-old girl named Benita Aguirre from Legazpi, approximately six miles southwest of Ezkioga. By August 1931, tens of thousands of people came to see her and other visionaries every day. Their visions were often so intense they fainted afterward and had to be carried down the mountain.

Pilgrims came from surrounding villages as well as cosmopolitan locales like Bilbao, Barcelona, Madrid, and Paris. Commoners and clergy alike ascended Ezkioga Mountain as believers or skeptics. Some switched sides upon making their visit. People came to witness for themselves what was happening: seers blessing crucifixes and rosaries and answering petitioners' questions about whether loved ones who'd passed away had made it out of Purgatory into Heaven. One seer claimed the baby Jesus had marked her with a dagger. Great excitement ensued when a scratch was found on her hand—until evidence suggested a razor had caused the wound. Some visionaries saw the dead, others saw the devil. Still, others saw witches—as Basques did amid the upheavals of the early seventeenth century, a fictionalized account of which can be found in my novel, *The Hammer of Witches*. For comparisons between the 1610 witch trials and the events at Ezkioga, see Christian's *Visionaries*, pages 211–213.

Detractors of the Ezkioga visions and seers were many. Chief among them was the Jesuit priest and popular scientist, Jose Antonio Laburu. He recorded the seers in vision on film—unfortunately, since lost—and concluded they did not meet the criteria for "true" visions, per Thomas Aquinas and Teresa de Avila. Condemning evidence included the seers' abilities to predict when their visions would occur, the childish nature of their requests while in vision, and the contrast in their behavior before and after their visions. Indeed, the Reverend Andoni Eizaguirre Galarraga quipped, "Whether the Virgin Mary appeared at Ezkioga we cannot say, but it is certain along the way there appeared numerous virgins and later baby Jesuses" (Christian 1996, 383). The original Basque reads: "*Ama Birgiña Ezkio'n azaldu zan edo ez/Iñork garbi ez dakigu/Bañan bai bide baztarretan ama birjin ugari agertu zirela/Eta ondoren amaika niño Jesus*" (Christian 1996, 468).

In December of 1931, the diocese forbade clergy from visiting the apparition site. Yet, the visions continued in earnest. By mid-January of 1932, seers were reenacting Christ's crucifixion during their visions, holding spectators in thrall. Believers built a small chapel on the vision site in October, predicting a shrine would grace the spot one day (as of this writing in 2024, the site still awaits its shrine.) By the end of 1933, seers themselves were prohibited from going to the apparition site. Republican forces started persecuting them in spring of 1934, considering the overt religiosity of the visions incongruent with the secular state they were attempting to create.

But, as Christian notes, it is too simplistic to say the visions were mere protests against the fledgling democratic republic. The seers of Ezkioga fought on both sides of the Spanish Civil War (1936–1939). Skepticism and persecution of the cult came from all sides. The Vatican issued a decree against the apparitions in 1934. Seers and believers went underground, yet they were not safe. Alleging the gatherings were but a breeding ground for Basque Nationalism, General Francisco Franco persecuted the seers and devotees from 1937 to 1941. When a new bishop arrived in Ezkioga in the 1940s, he reiterated the

Holy See's disapproval of the cult, and "visions were omitted in local histories" (Christian 1996, 378–382).

By the time Christian met them when they were in their eighties and nineties, believers were "[a]shamed of their own enthusiasm"; they and their families had born the "stigma of Ezkioga in total silence for sixty years" (Christian 1996, 400–401). The child seers lived with fear of discovery until their deaths. Benita Aguirre herself changed her name to Maria, got married, had a daughter, and moved to Madrid. She never revealed to her nanny/companion of almost forty years that she was the famous child seer of Ezkioga. A few years before she died, Benita burned all her personal papers, making sure the fire incinerated every scrap. Until her death, she continued to share messages from the divine with her devotees.

This rich context inspired *Apparitions*, and I am indebted to William Christian for his thorough research on the subject. But, this is ultimately a work of fiction. Though Benita has become "Blanca," her storyline comes primarily from my imagination. William is loosely based on Walter Starkie, a Hispanist/fiddler who visited Ezkioga in the summer of 1931. My descriptions of the apparition site, as well as of the characters Old Simon and Doña Carmen, are drawn in part from his 1934 memoir *Spanish Raggle Taggle: Adventures with a Fiddle in Northern Spain* (Murray 1934). Sofia's political philosophy was inspired by Dolores Ibarruri, known as "La Pasionaria," author of the often quoted but usually unattributed slogan: "They Shall Not Pass!" The lives of William and Sofia have nothing else to do with Walter and Dolores. None of the other characters is historical, so by definition nothing that happened to them ever really happened to anyone real.

Once again, we find ourselves in a time of upheaval and uncertainty around the world. As Old Simon might say: who is to say what might happen still?

ACKNOWLEDGMENTS

Mila esker bihotz-bihotzez to the following for their support as I wrote *Apparitions*: my writing teacher, Louella Nelson, and my fellow students, Susan Angard, Laurie Casey, Dennis Copeland, Herb Williams-Dalgart, Debra Garfinkel, Kristen James, Brad Oatman, Dennis Phinney, Bev Plass, and Judith Whitmore. I also wish to thank Susan Ossman, Jean Valjean Ramon, Annika Speer, and especially Margaret Nash. As always, Candida Echeverria provided me with sustenance and encouragement, for which I am grateful.

For those new to the Basque language, the following guide, *Basque-English Dictionary* by Gorka Aulestia, provides the standardized alphabet with approximate pronunciation in English (Aulestia 1989, a19).

a	*far*
b	*bat*
d	*down*
e	*get*
f	*favor*
g	*got*
h	*house*
I	*marine*
j	*hot; yet*
k	*king*
l	*league*
m	*mayo*
n	*narrow*
ñ	*onion*
o	*coat*
p	*people*
r	*bedding*
s	*sh*
t	*tea*
u	*boot*
x	*fish*
z	*miss*

Prologue

Depictions of Aranzibia Hill are based on descriptions and photographs in William Christian's *Visionaries: The Spanish Republic and the Reign of Christ* (University of California Press, 1996), and Walter Starkie's descriptions of the apparition site in Ezkioga in *Spanish Raggle Taggle: Adventures with a Fiddle in Northern Spain* (London: John Murray, 1934), 126–146.

Blanca's vision is based on Christian's *Visionaries: The Spanish Republic and the Reign of Christ* (University of California Press,1996), 353–358.

Chapter One

"Ignore the foolishness of this world": Based on *Argia*. August 30, 1931.

"Gaizkatu España:" *Euskadi*. July 15, 1931.

For more on The Presentation of Mary, see www.vaticannews.va.

For more on Hildegard von Bingen: www.fordham.edu/halsa11/med/hildegarde.html.

"Our Lady of Anboto" adapted from "A mother's curse": Jose Dueso, *Lamiak et Sorginak* (Donostia, Honena, 1998), 14. Translation by the late Alan R. King.

"There once lived two sisters...": Jose Miguel Barandiarán, *Brujería y Brujas* (San Sebastián: Txertoa, 2002), 92. Translation by the late Alan R. King.

Chapter Two

"Once upon a time . . .": Adapted from Jose Dueso, *Lamiak eta Sorginak* (Donostia: Honena, 1998), 14–15.

Himno de Riego: Lyrics by Evaristo Fernández de San Miguel (1820) and composition by José Melchor Gomis (1820).

Description of Old Simon: adapted from William Starkie, *Spanish Raggle Taggle: Adventures with a Fiddle in Northern Spain* (London: John Murray, 1934), 113.

"Herriko Besta Biharmunean": Jose Maria Iparragirre (1897).

Chapter Three

"Revolt Starts in Spain": *New York Times*. December 13, 1931.

Malkorra bakery still exists in Elizondo in the Baztan valley of Nafarroa (www.malkorra.com).

Chapter Four

"Jende Onak": Mostly my composition but some lines are taken from "Santa Agata": Patri Urkizu, *Lapurdi, Baxanabarre eta Zuberoako Bertso et Kantak 1* (Donostia-San Sebatian: Etor, 199s), 319–321; and "Saraka Martira, Madalena Larralde": Urkizu, *Lapurdi, Baxanabarre eta Zuberoako Bertso eta Kanta 1*, 380–381).

Bonbons inspired by Chocolatier Cazenave. 19 Rue Port Neuf Bayonne France 64100.

"Hemen sartzen dena" trunk: "Baionako armarriarekiko kafeontzi lokomotorea, bere orgattoarekin." J.B. Tosselli eta Konpainiaren, 1865ean Baionako franko-espainiar Erakusketan saritua. *Musee Basque et de l'histoire de Bayonne/Baionako Euskal Museoa*. Olivier Ribeon, Jacques Battesti, Maider Etchepare Jaureguy (Le Festin: 2008, 57).

Toy-train coffee carafe based on "Baionako armarriarekiko kafeontzi lokomotorea, bere orgattoarekin." J.B. Tosselli eta Konpainiaren, 1865ean Baionako franko-espainiar Erakusketan saritua. *Musee Basque et de l'histoire de Bayonne/Baionako Euskal Museoa*. Olivier Ribeon, Jacques Battesti, Maider Etchepare Jaureguy (Le Festin: 2008, 201).

Chapter Five

Fr. Itcea's notes on Immaculate Conception: Patrick P. McBrien, *The Harper Collins Encyclopedia of Catholicism* (San Francisco: Harper Collins, 1995), 655–656.

Fr. Itcea's notes and homily on Bernadette Soubirous: Catholic.org and Patrick P. McBrien, *The Harper Collins Encyclopedia of Catholicism* (San Francisco: Harper Collins, 1995), pgs. 80–81, 157–158.

"Atzo nurbait izan düzü ene ait'ametara": Julie Adrienne Carricaburu y Roger (Mme. De la Villehelio) (ed.), *Souvenir des Pyrenees, Recuerdo de los Pireneos: 12 Canciones Vascas Escogidas y Anotacas* (1869), 324–329.

"Or She will come again, holding a sword dripping in blood": See Christian, *Visionaries: The Spanish Republic and the Reign of Christ* (University of California Press, 1996), 55.

Chapter Six

"Nobility Celebrates King Alfonso's 'Name Day'": *New York Times*. January 23, 1931. For more on St. Ildefonsus, see Catholic.org.

"Girls Lead Protest in Spain": *New York Times*. March 26, 1931.

An account of "Mutil Dantza" with regard to the agotas can be found in: Julio Caro Baroja, *The Basques* (Center for Basque Studies at the University of Nevada, Reno: 2009), p. 297.

Chapter Seven

"Jende Onak": Mostly my composition but some lines taken from "Santa Agata": Patri Urkizu, *Lapurdi, Baxanabarre eta Zuberoako Bertso et Kantak 1* (Donostia-San Sebastian: Etor, 199s), 319–321; and "Saraka Martira, Madalena Larralde": Urkizu, *Lapurdi, Baxanabarre eta Zuberoako Bertso eta Kanta 1*, 380–381).

"Spain Held Ready to Turn Republican:" Jules Sauerwein. *New York Times*. December 25, 1930.

The details of Maria's case can be found in my first novel, *The Hammer of Witches* (Center for Basque Studies at the University of Nevada, Reno, 2014). For more information on the historical case that inspired my novel, see Gustav Henningsen, *The Witches' Advocate: Basque Witchcraft and the Spanish Inquisition (1609–1614)*. University of Nevada: Reno, 1980.

Ads for Fortificante express, FLIT, etc., taken from or inspired by these newspapers: *El Dia* 7/1931-3/1932; *Argia* 7/1931-10/1931; and *Euzkadi* 7/1931-8/1931.

"Beside the last of these": Based on photograph of "Carmen Girón Camino, described in the caption as 'Miss República and even better, Miss Spain," on cover of *Crónica* published July 12, 1931. See William A. Christian Jr., *Visionaries: The Spanish Republic and the Reign of Christ* (University of California Press: 1996, pg 98).

Chapter Eight

Father Itcea's Easter homily drawn in part from *Aranzazu*. September 16, 1931.

"Born to the purple . . .". Spain's Crown sits securely. John Steven McGroarty. *Los Angeles Times*. December 15, 1030: 2.

Chapter Nine

Blessed Mother's message to build a chapel comes from *Argia*. August 30, 1931.

Chapter Ten

Radio broadcast base don "King Alfonso XIII Quits": Frank L. Kluckhohn. *New York Times*. April 14, 1931.

La marseilles and translation adapted from: brittanica.com.

"Gernikako arbola": Jose Maria Iparragirre (1853).

Chapter Eleven

"Spain's steadiness amazes observer": Jules Sauerwein, *New York Times*. April 18, 1931: 8.

"Spain to negotiate church separation": Frank L. Kluckhohn, *New York Times*. April 18, 1931:

"After dropping steadily for nearly a week, the peseta," from "Decline in Peseta Since 1898." *New York Times*. June 27, 1930.

"Strikes in Andalusia have added . . ." from "Decline in Peseta Since 1898." *New York Times*. June 27, 1930.

"Jaingoikoa eta Lege Zaharra—God and the Old Laws" article: Adapted from *Aranzazu*. August 14, 1931 & September 16, 1931.

Cerquand, Jean-François. *Légendes et Récits Populaire du Pay Basque"—Legends and Popular Tales of the Basque Country* (Paris: Leon Ribaut, 1875–1876).

Chapter Twelve

"Arise fellow workers": Dolores Ibarruri, *They Shall Not Pass: Background and Story of the Spanish Civil War by the Heroic Resistance Leader* (International Publishers, 1966), 26.

Chapter Thirteen

L'Internationale: Eugène Pottier (1871).

Chapter Fourteen

For Maria's story, see *The Hammer of Witches: A Historical Novel* (University of Nevada Reno Center for Basque Studies, 2014).

"Churches Looted. Republicans Suspected:" *New York Times*. May 8, 1931.

"Move to Try Alfonso for Staging Anti-Monarchist Riots": *New York Times*. May 8, 1931.

"All shall be well": see julianofnorwich.org.

Chapter Fifteen

Sources for Fr. Itcea's Pentecost homily: catholicnewsagency and US Council of Catholic Bishops (www.usccb.org).

For instruction on "Metanoia," I am indebted to Michael Zampelli, SJ.

Chapter Sixteen

Sources for Fr. Itcea's list comparisons of Lourdes and Fatima include Patrick P. McBrien, *The Harper Collins Encyclopedia of Catholicism*, 80–81.

Sources for the apparitions in Knock, Ireland include McBrien, *The Harper Collins Encyclopedia of Catholicism*, 740.

Chapter Eighteen

Blanca's chastisement vision based on Christian's *Visionaries: The Spanish Republic and the Reign of Christ*: 357–358.

Blessed Mother's message based on Christian's *Visionaries: The Spanish Republic and the Reign of Christ*: 32.

Chapter Nineteen

"Maria, Aranzibian": Adapted from "Ezkio'ko Ama, lagun iguzu!" *Argia*. August 23, 1931.

Chapter Twenty

"The Republican Cabinet has decided to seize . . ." from "Spain to Confiscate Ex-King's . . .": *New York Times*. May 14, 1931.

Chapter Twenty-One

"Cantemos al amor" by Restituto del Valle (1865–1930).

"Soon there will be a time of great trials"from Christian, *Visionaries: The Spanish Republic and the Reign of Christ* (University of California Press, 1996), 323.

Afterward

Christian, William. 1996. *Visionaries: The Spanish Republic and the Reign of Christ.* Berkeley: University of California Press.

Echeverria, Begoña. 2014. *The Hammer of Witches.* Reno: University of Nevada Reno Center for Basque Studies.

Murray, John. *Spanish Raggle Taggle: Adventures with a Fiddle in Northern Spain.* London: printed by the author, 1934.

A pithy account based on Starkie's first-hand testimony and William Christian's scholarship can be found in: Chris Maunder, "Basque Raggle-Taggle: Ezkioga," in *Our Lady of the Nations: Apparitions of Mary in Twentieth Century Catholic Europe* (Oxford University Press: 2016), 74–83.

For excellent reportage on Spain between 1930–1931, I recommend *New York Times'* writers Frank L. Kluckhohn, Anne O'Hare McCormick, Clair Price, and Jules Sauerwein.

Aulestia, Gorka. 1989. *Basque-English Dictionary.* Reno: University of Nevada Reno Center for Basque Studies.

I am grateful for the above writers and sources for the historical background, context, and archival materials they provided. I have endeavored to do them justice.